WHAT PEOPLE
DANIEL HENSH

CW00859779

BOOKS BY DANIEL HENSHAW

GLENKILLY

DANIEL HENSHAW

First published 2020

ISBN 9798646811906

Cover artwork and illustrations by Jimmy Rogers
booyeah.co.uk
Twitter: @jimmyrogers

For Alan, King of the Peanuts.
Thank you for everything.
Hope this is not too scary for you!

MONDAY

CHAPTER ONE:
UNLUCKY FOR SOME

I had a feeling we were in Scotland. The sky had darkened, the fields were full of hairy Highland cattle and I'd seen a big sign that said *'Welcome to Scotland'*.

We were here for camping, which sounded scary enough – with the breeze and the bats and the bagpipes – but my nervousness increased with each mile as I watched the terrifying scenery through the coach window. The Scottish countryside was full of danger. Armies of dark pine trees stood in great clumps, as if they were hiding some chilling secret, and – in the far distance – huge, deadly mountains were half-hidden by swirling clouds. The safety of towns and people had quickly become a distant memory.

There was a stinky, stale atmosphere on the coach – all bad breath and boredom – and for hours on end, I'd been squished between the window and my best friend, Michael. He'd taken the aisle seat, claiming to have a *'window allergy'*, which sounded far-fetched, even for him.

"Aren't you worried?" I asked, despite knowing that Michael never worried.

He arched a casual eyebrow. "About what?"

"This trip. We're camping in the middle-of-nowhere."

"You don't need to worry, Jeremy. Just relax."

"*Relax?* How can I relax? Have you not seen the size of those cows' horns? How are we meant to defend ourselves? We're only ten."

"They're just cows, Jeremy."

I shook my head. "And what about today's date?"

Michael shrugged, secretly scoffing the bag of *Mini Cheddars* that our teacher, Mr Hopton, had specifically told him not to open. "October?" he eventually said.

"October the *thirteenth*," I added.

"So what?"

"The *thirteenth*. Thirteen is an unlucky number."

Michael looked at me blankly. "Is it?"

"Yes! My mum says that bad things always happen on Friday the thirteenth."

"But, Jeremy, it's Monday."

"And she says that the skyscrapers in New York don't have a thirteenth floor because it's such a bad omen. *Thirteen. Unlucky for some.* That's what Mum always says."

I sighed, my breath fogging the glass as I scanned for danger outside. The bumpy country roads had narrowed now and dark trees towered over us, draping the coach in a blanket of shadows.

"I've never been camping before," I admitted. "What if I can't do any of the activities?"

Michael laughed. Finishing his *Mini Cheddars,* he screwed up the packet before wiping his fingers on his tracky bottoms. "Come on, mate. You'll be fine. You're good at *some* things. Like that picture of a wasp you drew. That was… *alright.*"

"Thanks mate."

I smiled, though I wasn't quite sure how useful a drawing of a wasp would be on a school camping trip. Still, I bent my arm and pointed my elbow. Michael did the same and we gently tapped elbows. It was our special thing. We'd always wanted a secret handshake but couldn't do any of the complicated ones we'd seen on YouTube. So we had the Elbow-Bump instead.

Our coach then slowed right down and our driver flicked on the indicator as the roadside trees parted to reveal an electric gate in the middle of a tall iron fence. It didn't look like the entrance to a campsite, more like a prison, or worse, a school.

The gate suddenly jolted, before slowly... very, very slowly... sliding open, as though unsure about letting us in. Once inside, a long, winding drive led up a small hill towards a gloomy building on the horizon, silhouetted black against the grey October sky.

Although the place was named Glenkilly Castle, the building barely resembled a *castle* at all. There was no moat or drawbridge, no turrets or cannons. It was more like a stately manor house with gleaming windows running along the walls, like a hundred square eyes, and ghastly gargoyles glaring down from the roof.

Stepping off the stifling coach, the cool Scottish air felt heavenly against my grubby skin. The autumn sky was grey and sunless and it already felt too cold for camping.

There were twenty of us on the trip altogether, along with our teachers, Mr Hopton and Mrs Dodd, and we gathered by the side of the coach as the driver passed us our belongings. I thought *my* bag was over-packed but Michael's enormous red rucksack was so heavy he almost toppled over when he put it on his back. Every time he moved, it rattled like a tin of marbles and I couldn't begin to imagine what was in it.

We then headed towards the castle, everyone chatting merrily as our feet crunched across the gravel car park. And that's when we spotted the badger.

Now, I'd seen some pretty disturbing things during my first ten years on Earth – men with hairy backs, steaming cow pats, Auntie Carol's lasagne – but this was the worst. The badger lay at the edge of the car park, stiff as a board, its eyes glazed over. Weird bald patches ran across its back, where a gang of squabbling magpies were greedily pecking at the poor thing's flesh. And, yuckiest of all, blood spattered from its mouth as though it had swallowed a whole bottle of ketchup before throwing up.

"You think it's dead?" said Michael.

"Looks pretty dead to me."

No one else had noticed it.

"Should we tell Mr Hopton?" I asked.

Michael shook his head. "Nah. He'll only panic."

In all honesty, glaring down at the poor animal, having its guts nibbled by magpies, *I* was starting to panic. What sort of place was this, where they leave dead animals lying around for children to see?

"I used to have a pet badger," said Michael.

I didn't respond. Michael had a habit of bending the truth. He once told me he'd seen a goat driving a Ford Fiesta through Asda car park. How its hooves were supposed to have reached the pedals, I really don't know.

"What do you think killed it?" I asked as we moved away, crossing the car park towards a paved path at the front of the castle.

"Probably a wolf," said Michael.

My nerves tightened. "Do they have wolves in Scotland?"

Michael nodded. "I saw one on the way up here."

"You never mentioned it. And you didn't even sit near the window."

He didn't answer.

As we approached the castle's big wooden doors, I noticed something rather odd. Other than the excited chit-chat of our classmates, everything else here seemed quiet... too quiet, like in a doctor's waiting room, or a maths test. I couldn't see any other school groups. No children racing around, no teachers being forced onto the zip-line... nobody at all. Weird.

As we climbed the stone steps in front of the wooden doors, the coach hissed behind us before rumbling into action. I glanced around to see it heading back towards the electric gate, its noisy engine startling the greedy magpies. They scattered in an explosion of black and white feathers, flying off to perch on a nearby telephone line.

I counted them silently.

Thirteen magpies.

Thirteen.

Unlucky for some.

CHAPTER TWO: JUST JEREMY

The castle had a musty smell – of wood and leather – and it reminded me of *The Horse and Jockey,* where I sometimes went for a carvery with Mum.

We were ushered into a warm sitting room filled with old leather sofas, varnished coffee tables and a stained tartan carpet. A cosy log fire hissed and crackled inside a grand stone fireplace, which had a coat of arms impressively carved into it and a huge antique clock on the mantelpiece.

Portraits of miserable old men lined the wood-panelled walls and a rusty suit of armour stood motionless in one corner like a frozen robot. A massive stag's head hung above the door and I wondered how long ago the animal had died. Five years ago? Fifty? Five hundred? Maybe they'd have the badger on the wall next week.

"Hi, guys! Welcome to Glenkilly Castle."

The voice came from a tall man standing by the fireplace. He spoke with a Scottish accent so smooth he could have been an airline pilot. Although well into his forties, the man had a diamond stud in his ear, teeth bright enough to be seen from outer space and skin so orange he reminded me of… well, an orange.

"My name's Hamish, and this is Kat."

By his side, stood a youngish lady, with a trendy pair of spectacles framing her eyes. Like Hamish, she grinned an enormous grin, though her teeth were a more natural shade of white.

"Hi, everybody." Kat spoke in a high-pitched, pixie voice. Waves of orange hair curled down past her shoulders and a million orange freckles were scattered across her nose and cheeks. "We're your activity leaders here at Glenkilly," she said. "And we're looking forward to a fun, fantastic week with you all."

Both Kat and Hamish wore green uniforms with the words *GLENKILLY STAFF* stitched into their jackets. They gave a quick speech about moving safely around the grounds and mentioned some of the exciting/slightly terrifying activities we'd be doing this week: canoeing, zip-lining, go-karting. They also warned us not to drink the tap water, because they were having problems with the plumbing, so each of us was given a bottle of Highland mineral water and a shortbread biscuit.

Once they'd finished talking, I shuffled over to a huge bay window with Michael. Looking out, I saw fields running for miles around – as though the castle were floating on a sea of green – and further away from the building stood the black forest, like a shadowy perimeter fence, surrounding the grounds on all sides.

As I nibbled a biscuit, I was about to ask Michael which activities he was looking forward to when something peculiar caught my eye. Poking its head above the woodland, I spotted a tall metal structure, a bit like a giant tower of scaffolding. Hundreds of pine trees huddled tightly around it, like bodyguards protecting an important leader.

"What's that?" I asked, pointing out of the window.

Michael peered past me. "Looks like the Eiffel Tower."

I raised an eyebrow but said nothing. Something about the tower made me uneasy. What was it? Some sort of extreme climbing cage?

Thanks to the creepy castle and the dead badger and now this strange tower, I felt jittery. Michael wouldn't get it. He never worried about anything. Usually I'd go to Mum for reassurance but she was a billion-trillion miles away, back home. Across the room, I spotted Kat standing alone. She seemed nice, so I headed towards her, squeezing past my classmates through the crowded room while Michael stayed by the window.

"Howdy," I said as an introduction. I'm not sure why. The moment the word left my mouth, it sounded ridiculous and I silently vowed to never, ever say 'howdy' again for the rest of my life.

Kat looked down at me and smiled. I noticed a small hoop pierced into her nose and a rainbow of cotton bracelets wrapped around her wrist. *Hippie Bracelets.* That's what Dad would've called them.

"Hello there," Kat answered, her voice pillow soft. She lowered her head towards me, and I caught the sweet scent of her perfume, like fresh flowers. "What can I do for you?"

"Hi, um…" I suddenly felt nervous for some reason. "My name's Jeremy. Jeremy Green. But people call me… just Jeremy."

"Hello, Just Jeremy."

"No, it's just… Jeremy."

"Okay, Just… Jeremy. What can I do for you?"

I frowned, unsure what to make of her. "Um… well, could you tell me what that tower is in the middle of the forest?"

Her eyes shifted around the room. "The tower? That's, erm… nothing to worry about. Did you get a biscuit? And a bottle of water?"

I raised my empty bottle, noting that she hadn't actually answered my question. "I also saw a badger. Near the car park. Just as we were coming in."

Kat's face brightened. "Oh, that's great. There's plenty of wonderful wildlife for you guys to see around here. You're quite lucky to see a badger though. They're actually nocturnal."

"It was dead."

"Oh."

"Its skin had come off and magpies were eating it."

Kat's eyes widened in horror and the colour drained from her face. "Oh, erm…" She glanced at Hamish – but he was busy telling Mr Hopton about the cereals available at breakfast.

"Right," said Kat, turning back to me. She nervously tucked a strand of orange hair behind her ear. "Well. There's no need to panic."

"I'm not."

"It's just the circle of life, you know. Sadly, animals die all the time. It may have been hit by a car or perhaps it was just old. I'm so sorry. You weren't supposed to see that."

Kat smiled – though her anxious eyes never changed.

You weren't supposed to see that.

What did that mean? Her worried expression told me that she wasn't being honest. But what exactly was she hiding?

Kat smiled again, before turning back to Hamish and taking him by the arm. She delicately moved him away from Mr Hopton.

Not wanting to miss out, I stepped closer.

"That weird kid over there says he saw a dead badger," Kat murmured. "With *skin* missing."

Weird kid? What did she mean?

Hamish sighed, scratching the stubble on his chin. "They weren't supposed to see any of that. Go and shift it."

Kat nodded before darting from the room.

Those words again.

They weren't supposed to see any of that.

Now my head was abuzz with questions. Why were they so bothered about a dead badger? Why did they not want us to see it? Why would a man in his forties wear a diamond stud in his ear?

Then my insides shrivelled – because, judging by the way that Hamish was glaring at me, I realised I'd just asked all of those questions… out loud!

Weird Kid.

CHAPTER THREE:
ROTTING RABBITS

"Jeremy Green! Pay attention!"

Our teacher, Mr Hopton, had a nasally voice like a strangled goat. It snapped me from a daydream as an icy wind whistled through the archery range and grey clouds hovered above. Having set up camp – shoving our bags into a tent and laying out our sleeping bags – we were now crowded around Hamish, the walking midlife-crisis.

"Whenever you're loading your bow, guys," the activity leader was saying, "keep the arrow pointing away from your friends, preferably towards the floor or the target."

"Safety is extremely important!" Mr Hopton bleated.

"Make sure the nock fits onto the bow, guys, just beneath the nocking point." He placed the arrow onto the bow.

I hadn't been listening so I had no idea what a 'nock' was – or a 'nocking point'.

"You'll know when it's in the right place, guys, because you'll hear it click."

Something clicked.

"Pull the string all the way back to your cheek. And then release." He let go of the string and the arrow flashed to the target, hitting the yellow circle in the middle. Everyone clapped.

When it was my turn, I followed Hamish's advice. I tried to pull the string right back and keep my arms steady and all the rest of it, but my first shot failed to even reach the target. Connor McCafferty sniggered as my arrow nestled pathetically into the grass. I turned around to scowl but Connor – his black fringe almost hiding his eyes – was whispering something to the other boys before pointing at me. A chorus of cackles followed, causing my face to glow.

Connor thought he was the *Bad Boy* of the class. With a black stud in each ear, he wrote rude words on tables, stuck chewing gum on teachers' cardigans, and walked on the grass when there were clear signs that said, '*Do Not Walk on the Grass*.' His black hair hung below his ears, often covering half of his face. He seemed to think this gave him an air of mystery, like a rock star or a James Bond villain. But really, he just looked like one of those dogs that can't see because of its overgrown fringe.

By the time I'd finished my six shots, not a single arrow had reached the target. I tried to blame the wind but nobody listened.

"Nice one, *Jellyfish*," Connor sneered.

More laughter from the crowd.

He'd been calling me *'Jellyfish'* ever since we learned about them in class.

A jellyfish doesn't have a brain.

A jellyfish doesn't have a heart.

Some jellyfish are invisible to the human eye.

He's only jealous, Mum always said, which was pretty hard to believe as I'd just watched him hit a tiny yellow archery target with six arrows. *Just ignore him,* were Mum's other words of wisdom, which was also pretty hard to do when everyone in class laughed along with him.

Then I remembered Dad's words. *Man up.*

I felt my nostrils flare.

Clenching my fists, I stepped towards Connor, ready to take him down.

But it was no use.

Without flinching, Connor straightened, towering over me, his dead, shark-like, brown eyes glaring from behind his black fringe.

Like a true wimp – a person who was afraid of mud and moths and men in kilts – I instinctively cowered, skulking in fear like the Hunchback of Notre Dame.

Man up?

More like 'man down'.

Defeated, I retook my spot at the back of the crowd… as far from Connor as possible.

Jellyfish have no backbone.

I huffed. Archery was stupid anyway. It wasn't like anyone needed to shoot arrows these days, was it?

No longer interested in this pointless activity, I gazed around at the grounds. Glenkilly Castle stood such a distance from the archery range, it looked like a tiny bungalow from here, surrounded by acres of green fields, all penned in by the forest.

I was about to turn back to the archery when my eye caught on an odd shape in the grass nearby; some sort of animal. Stepping away from the archery range, I moved towards the mysterious object. The creature lay perfectly still, about the size of a small cat, with light brown and greyish fur.

I crept closer.

Again, it didn't move.

Was it sleeping? Injured, perhaps?

I took one more step… before realising it was…

Urgh! A dead rabbit!

My mind flashed to the badger.

Two dead animals in such a short space of time.

I'd seen a dead pigeon in town once but this was far worse. Like the badger, most of the rabbit's fur had fallen out. I could even see some of its bones, with tiny insects crawling all over the remains.

A cheer from the archery range disturbed my observations. But as I was turning back to my classmates, I noticed a second animal about five metres away. Curious, I wandered over to the small clump of brown fur. Sure enough, it was another lifeless rabbit – a second scrawny body, chunks of hair missing in a similar way with hundreds of little bugs invading the poor rabbit's flesh.

Peering across the grass, I noticed a third rabbit, missing fur, just the same.

Then a fourth.

And a fifth.

I felt like Hansel, or Gretel (whichever one was the boy), but instead of a breadcrumb trail, I had a trail of rotting rabbits to find my way back.

But why so many dead bunnies?

I stepped over to a sixth carcass, and before I knew it, I'd trekked across an entire field and was standing at the edge of the black woods.

Staring into the tangle of trees and bushes and branches and leaves, I couldn't help but notice how dark and eerie it looked inside the forest. Even in the middle of the afternoon, the woodland was draped in sinister black shadows, making it hard to see anything clearly.

I glanced down at the sixth rabbit, missing so much hair it was almost bald. What could possibly have happened? The rabbits didn't look like they'd been attacked. But it was strange how they all looked so similar. All skinny, all hairless, all… dead. And their trail had led me to this spot at the edge of the gloomy woods, where an overly-sweet scent hung in the air. It smelled like the flowery jasmine air-freshener my mum used, though I couldn't see any flowers in the woods.

I was turning to leave when…

Crack!

What was that? A snapping twig? Was someone there?

Staring into the dark forest, my eyes fixed on a set of branches jutting out from a tree. They looked sharp and dangerous and, for a moment, I thought they could be antlers.

I tried to focus. With all the shadows, I couldn't tell whether my eyes were playing tricks on me… but something looked to be moving, just ever so slightly. Breathing, maybe? My heart hammered so hard, I could practically hear it.

And then I froze, barely daring to breathe myself, as I realised what I was seeing.

There, about ten metres ahead, half-hidden behind the trunk of a wide tree, someone – or some*thing* – was staring right at me… with bright red eyes.

CHAPTER FOUR:
WED-EYED MONSTER

Something crashed through the undergrowth, snapping branches and twigs. I froze, staring at the woods and the blur of movement ahead, fearing that my life was about to end...

But then, almost instantly, everything was still again.

The red-eyed creature was gone.

"Jeremy!"

I jumped as Mr Hopton's voice shrieked through the cold air behind me.

"Jeremy!" He was marching towards me in his faded yellow tracksuit. "What do you think you're playing at?"

"We're playing archery, aren't we?"

"Not in those woods we're not. What are you doing all the way over here?"

Even *I* thought Mr Hopton was a total stress-head. He fretted about everything. We couldn't even use glue sticks in class without him lecturing us for thirty minutes about the dangers of eating them or sticking them in our ears.

I was about to answer his question but he didn't give me chance.

"There are all sorts of dangers in those woods! Nettles, thistles… ladybirds! Anything could've happened to you! Now let's get back to the others." He lowered his voice to a much gentler tone. "I know that archery isn't one of your strengths, Jeremy, but there's no need to sulk. When is quitting ever a good idea?"

"Erm… smoking."

"What?"

"Quitting smoking is a good idea."

Mr Hopton frowned. His blotchy skin was dry and red, and his wispy hair barely covered his balding scalp. "Well, yes," he said eventually. "Quitting smoking *is* a good idea, obviously, but that's not what I meant. Now, come on, we need to get back."

As I followed him to the archery range, he didn't even notice the rabbit corpses.

"But Mr Hopton, there's a dead –"

"There's a dead good chance you'll get a bullseye next time, Jeremy."

"No, Mr Hopton. I think there's something in the woods."

"Yes Jeremy, there's a lot of wet grass and if you'd gone any further, you could have slipped over and scratched your arm and then I'd have to fill in an Accident Form."

"Scratched my arm? No, Mr Hopton, I saw –"

"Jeremy, *I saw* you shoot some very good arrows earlier."

A definite lie.

"Now, the competition has started and it's your turn next."

"But Mr Hopton, there was something –"

"Even Mrs Dodd has some points on the board, so I'm sure you can manage it." He winked after saying this.

Mrs Dodd was our other teacher on the trip, a rodenty woman with buck-teeth and poodle-like greying hair. Her sharp, narrow eyes were framed by a thick pair of specs and were always full of suspicion.

"It makes you wonder," was something she *always* said, though I was never quite sure what we were supposed to be 'wondering' about.

Reluctantly rejoining the group, I watched Mr Hopton whisper something into to Mrs Dodd's ear.

"It makes you wonder," she muttered, shaking her head.

They obviously weren't going to listen to me, so I took matters into my own hands.

"THERE'S A MONSTER IN THE WOODS!" I announced, pointing at the trees.

My classmates stared at me with worried eyes and frowns etched across their foreheads. I heard titters of amusement too.

Mr Hopton flashed me a furious glare. "Jeremy, what on earth are you talking about?"

Connor McCafferty sniggered before adopting a baby voice. "Mummy, there's a monster in my bed-woom!"

Cackles of laughter rippled through the group.

My cheeks glowed. "It's true! It had these great big antlers and –"

"Antlers?" said Hamish, smooth as ever. "Young man, I think you've been lucky enough to see a stag."

"Yes, Jeremy," Mr Hopton screeched. "It was just a stag.

Now... *CALM DOWN!"*

"It wasn't a stag," I whimpered. "It was standing on two legs like a human or... or... a bear!"

"Pweeease, Mummy, save me fwom the monster!"

More laughter.

"Shush, Connor!" snapped Mr Hopton. "Jeremy, I don't think stags can stand on two legs."

27

"It wasn't a stag! It was standing upright and…" I took a deep breath. "… it had shiny, red eyes."

There were a few gasps and everyone was quiet for a moment. Hamish suddenly looked uneasy, scratching the back of his neck.

Connor broke the silence. "Pweeease, Mummy, it's the wed-eyed monster!" This fired up the laughter again. Then Connor's usual voice returned. "You really *are* a jellyfish, aren't you? No sign of a brain whatsoever."

"That's enough!" barked Mr Hopton. "I think it's time we forget all about this nonsense and get on with the archery contest."

"But –"

Mr Hopton's deadly glare silenced me.

I shuffled back into the crowd, feeling every single eye on me. People inched away, giving me a wide berth. I was clearly a weirdo, someone with issues, best to be avoided in case they caught the Weirdo Disease too.

Michael gave me a curious look and hesitated before Elbow-Bumping me. He'd opted out of the archery competition, saying he still felt sick from the coach journey. On the way here, his skin colour had changed from brown to an interesting shade of green before he'd spewed an interesting shade of orange... all over Mr Hopton's tracksuit.

Maybe I was a bit sick too. Maybe that's why I thought I'd seen something in the woods. Maybe that's why I was so bad at archery. No, that was just me.

As the contest restarted, Hamish returned his focus to the safe use of bows and arrows, occasionally giving children advice on how to improve. But every now and then, I saw him glance my way. He looked concerned, uncomfortable.

I knew I'd seen something strange in those woods; a creature with antlers and glowing red eyes, standing on its hind legs. Everyone else had laughed and Hamish had brushed it off as a stag. But something told me that Hamish *knew* I was telling the truth. The *thing* I'd seen... was *not* a stag.

CHAPTER FIVE:
OLD HABITS DIE HARD

Something had *definitely* been in those woods. Something strange had *definitely* happened to those rabbits. Something was *definitely* wrong with my bow.

After five rounds of arrows, I'd scored just twenty-seven points. Connor finished with a hundred and thirty-five. The only person who could beat him was Nazirah Hameed. She had three arrows left and a score of a hundred and six, meaning she needed three tens to win. Pretty unlikely.

I liked Nazirah. She was the smartest girl in our school by a million miles. She knew everything about everything. Even boring stuff like poetry and politics and professional snooker.

I used to love sitting next to Nazirah in maths. She'd always help me without making me feel stupid – and when I still didn't understand, she'd let me copy her answers. Which was great until our teacher at the time, Mr Chung, pointed out that we were meant to be solving completely different problems (Nazirah doing harder ones, obviously), so *all* of my answers were wrong. I didn't let this upset me though; apparently, five out of three people struggle with numbers.

Nazirah always wore a purple scarf – a hijab – around her head and shoulders because she followed the religion of Islam. Nazirah once told me that she didn't have to wear the hijab at home, only when she left the house. I'd said, "Well, I only have to a coat when I leave the house, so I guess that's the same." She laughed (for some reason), saying that it wasn't the same at all.

Right now, as Nazirah pulled back the bow string, her serious eyes focused on the target. She held the arrow for a moment, then released. Dead centre! Ten points!

Nazirah loaded the second arrow. Another ten! Everyone cheered and clapped. One more ten and she'd win the trophy. Even a nine would put her joint-first. I noticed Connor sulking at the thought of the competition being snatched away from him.

Come on Nazirah!

She loaded her final arrow in total silence. Everyone held their breath. Focusing on the target, Nazirah gripped her bow steady... pulled back the string... held it for a moment... until...

A blood-curdling scream pierced the silence!

Everyone flinched, including Nazirah, who jerked as she released the arrow, firing wildly into the air, missing the target and almost hitting a blue tit.

We all turned to see a tall, blonde girl named Imogen Rutherford, standing on the grass by the archery range. Her face was pale and twisted as she glared down at one of the rotting rabbits. Mr Hopton flapped and fussed, finally seeing the trail of dead animals.

Even Hamish's carrot-skin visibly paled. "Not again," he said. "I'm so sorry, guys. I'm so sorry. You weren't supposed to see those."

Those words again!

You weren't supposed to see those.

What did it mean?

Meanwhile, Mr Hopton was completely beside himself. "There could be all kinds of germs on those carcasses," he wailed, ushering everyone away. "Everybody listen! The air is contaminated with harmful bacteria. We need to stop breathing!"

We all looked at each other, confused.

"We can't *stop* breathing," said Nazirah, looking totally flummoxed.

"Good point," Mr Hopton admitted. "Okay. Don't *stop* breathing. *Keep* breathing but cover your mouths with your sleeves. Breathe into your clothes. It's the best way to avoid infection."

Grimacing, we covered our mouths as we walked back to camp.

"I'm so sorry, guys," Hamish said again as we returned to our tents. "It must be the house dog, Buster. Probably on one of his walks. He's an old Bloodhound, a hunting dog. He still goes after rabbits and grouse. I guess old habits die hard."

"And those rabbits died *hard*," said Connor, grinning.

"That's enough of that talk," snapped Mr Hopton.

When we reached our tents, Hamish apologised again before presenting Connor with the archery trophy. The smirk that stretched across his face made me want to puke. If it hadn't been for Imogen's squeal, Nazirah might have won instead.

"Bad luck," I said to her. "You deserved to win."

Nazirah smiled. "Thanks, Jeremy."

"Yeah," said Michael. "You'd have won if Imogen hadn't found those rabbits."

"I found them first," I said proudly. "That's why I wandered off. The rabbits led me to the woods. That's where I saw the... *thing*."

"Are you sure it wasn't Buster you saw?" asked Nazirah. "The Bloodhound?"

I shook my head. "It had antlers."

"Like a reindeer?" said Michael. "I've seen reindeer before, when we lived in the North Pole."

I ignored the fact that Michael had never lived in the North Pole. He used to live near an *Iceland* supermarket but that's not the same.

"It *could* have been a reindeer," I said, "but the antlers looked sharp. And its eyes were glowing red." I shrugged. "I don't know. It was dark. Maybe it was nothing. Did you see the rabbits though?"

Nazirah shook her head.

"I did," said Michael. "They had massive bite marks in them, like they'd been attacked by a wolf!"

They didn't.

"They were really skinny," I said, ignoring Michael. "And their hair had fallen out too."

A cold wind blew across the campsite as the sky darkened. I shuddered at the thought of those poor creatures. Hamish had blamed the dog, Buster, but something about his apologies didn't feel right. What had he said again?

You weren't supposed to see those.

What did it mean?

So many questions.

Was the thing I'd seen in the woods really breathing? Was it really watching? Had it really been there at all?

My mind scrambled to put these oddities together, to make sense of them – but, just like in maths class with Nazirah, I struggled to add it all up.

CHAPTER SIX:
EVIL BLACK SYRUP

What happened after dinner was like all of my worst nightmares rolled into one. I should've known how things were going to pan out when they served up a disappointing meal of soggy, pale chips and *haggis* on pizza. It was clearly a sign.

But far more alarming than the food, by the time we'd finished eating, *darkness* hung over the grounds of Glenkilly… and darkness worried me. Absolutely anything could be hiding in the shadows at night: a robber, a rat, a red-eyed monster.

At home, Mum kept the landing light on at bedtime, which helped me feel safe, but that sort of comfort was long forgotten at Glenkilly. And to make matters far more dangerous, we were now marching into the pitch-black forest, with nothing but moonlight and dodgy torches to guide the way.

We followed a camp-leader named Zach, a young man with black, shoulder-length hair and tattoos creeping from beneath the sleeves of his green jacket. He wore dark makeup around his eyes and his bottom lip was pierced with a silver ring. He reminded me of Edward Scissorhands from the creepy movie and, although Zach's hands looked perfectly human, his fingernails were painted black and he had a leather strap around his wrist with vicious metal spikes sticking out of it.

Annoyingly... Zach was also related to Connor. When the long-haired camp-leader had arrived to collect us, Connor had hugged him, shouting, "Zach is my cousin!" over and over and over again, loud enough for the people of Southern Somalia to hear.

"Tonight we're singing campfire songs," Zach had announced, speaking in a surprisingly gentle voice. "We have a huge fire ready in the woods. Let's go."

And off we went into the frighteningly dark forest, blindly following, our torchlights moving and bobbing as we walked. Sinister shadows constantly changed shape, stretching and shortening and tricking my eyes into seeing things that weren't really there. Eerie silhouettes of angry animals and ghastly creatures would appear and then vanish. Connor let out ghoulish howls and birdlike screeches, causing squeals amongst the girls and scowls from Mr Hopton.

"Is your cousin a punk rocker or something?" Imogen Rutherford asked as we stumbled through the woods.

Imogen – a super-rich, super-annoying girl – was the one who'd screamed when she saw the rabbits. She had perfectly-straightened blonde hair, perfectly long legs that seemed to go all the way up to her armpits and the most perfectly fake smile in the whole world.

She was the unofficial leader of a small group that Michael and I had nicknamed *The Girly, Whirly, Twirly Gang.* All members of the 'gang' were pretty and rich and obsessed with things that made them feel grown-up, like mobile phones and makeup and movies about hunky vampires.

"Mummy says I shouldn't go anywhere near punk rockers," she added, "because they don't wash their hair and they stink."

"I used to be a punk rocker," said Michael.

"Zach is *not* a punk rocker," Connor growled. "He's actually a goth."

"What's a goth?" Michael whispered.

"I think he's like an ugly butterfly," I replied.

"No," said Nazirah. "That's a moth. Goths are people with a dark fashion sense. Black clothes, black hair, black nail varnish. Goth culture began in the 1980s, taking influences from gothic literature and films."

"Thanks for the lecture," Connor scoffed, pretending to yawn. "History geek."

Just then, I noticed an opening in the trees and the bright glow of the campfire. Kat – the activity leader whose orange hair matched the flames – was poking at the fire with a stick, smiling as she welcomed us.

By Kat's side stood a dog.

"This is Buster," she said. "Come and say hello." She then lowered her voice to a pretend whisper. "Don't worry, his farts are worse than his bite."

Everyone chuckled... apart from me... as I remembered that Hamish had blamed the dog for killing those poor rabbits. I'd found it hard to believe at the time and now I was very dubious.

As we sat down on logs placed around the campfire, the old Bloodhound – with his brown, droopy face – padded lazily between us, enjoying strokes and friendly pats. Seeing his sad wet eyes, I found it hard to imagine how something as gentle and slow as Buster could have attacked those rabbits. To be honest, I found it hard to imagine how something as gentle and slow as Buster could make it to his breakfast bowl. He looked like a cross between a Bloodhound and a slug.

When he passed us, I ran my fingers across his soft back and, to my surprise, the fur became sharp and bristly in places. There were bald patches scattered across his back.

Was he ill? Did he need a vet?

Then I remembered the rabbits. They had fur missing too. So did the badger! What was going on here? Were all the animals at Glenkilly sick? Or had Buster caught a disease from biting the rabbits?

Before I had chance to worry any more, Kat told us all to stand and, moments later, we were singing silly songs with actions and clapping. We sang about bananas and a goldfish called Bob. We even jigged around to something called 'The Camel Dance'. Soon everyone was laughing and smiling and I'd practically forgotten that we were in the middle of a sinister forest with nothing but darkness around us for miles and miles.

Then, after an hour of chanting ridiculous songs and sharing amusing jokes (half of which didn't even make sense), Connor's cousin took centre stage.

"We're now going further into the woods," Zach announced. "Follow me. And if you dare, turn off your torches."

Mr Hopton sprang to his feet, panic plastered all over his face. "But keep them on if you can't see properly! We don't want any accidents!"

Half the class turned off their torches, giving the trees a deeper darkness, the shadows now a threatening shade of inky black. As we crept through the wet mulch of fallen leaves, the air felt colder with each step – as if we'd crossed into an icier climate.

With hardly any vision of the forest around us, my mouth felt dry. People whimpered, clearly petrified, while others were literally crying. Why didn't Mr Hopton put a stop to this? He clearly wasn't happy out here in the cold, barely able to see.

My breathing tightened. I felt more terrified than the time Imogen's poodle chased me down Clacton Close. Every hint of a breeze made me flinch. Every rustle of leaves sent my heart into a frenzy. I couldn't shake the feeling that the... *thing* might be lurking in the darkness beyond our torchlight.

Then a new sound filled the air; a trickle of water. At first, I thought it might be a small stream – but as we stepped deeper into the woods, the noise grew and grew until it gradually became the raspy hiss of a rushing river.

The trees parted and the moving water appeared, carving its way through the forest. In the darkness, the running water looked like evil black syrup, snaking past us like a liquid conveyor belt, never stopping, as if it wanted someone to fall in – just so it could drag them away.

Zach stopped by the water's edge and waited for us to gather around. As the moonlight broke through the clouds, it gave the water a hint of sparkle. We huddled together like a troop of terrified penguins, wondering what might happen next.

Zach placed the torch beneath his chin, giving his face a pale, ghastly appearance, like a ghoulish skeleton… or a school teacher.

"It's finally time to tell you the truth," he said as a sinister grin slithered across his pale face. "Glenkilly Castle has a deep, dark secret."

CHAPTER SEVEN:
SMELL OF THE DEVIL

I had no explanation for what happened by the river that night. I had no explanation for the strange powers that appeared to be summoned from another world. Deep into the pitch-black forest – with only slices of moonlight and the odd torch to help us see – Something mysterious clearly hung in the air at Glenkilly.

"Ewww!" Michael murmured. "What's that smell?"

That wasn't *quite* what I meant – but a nasty, eggy stench was practically melting our nostril hairs. Not even the cold October breeze seemed to be blowing it away.

"Smells like a gas leak," I groaned, pinching my nose.

"Hang on a sec," said Michael.

I waited in silence… waiting for Michael to say something wise and profound… and then… his bottom erupted with a loud ripple. "Now that's what I call a gas leak!"

Giggling, we then Elbow-Bumped.

"It's the smell of the devil," whispered Connor, a terrible twist of delight stretching across his smug face. Wearing his long black coat and his long black hair, Connor reminded me of a raven… the symbol of death. "Something horrible is about to happen."

This made me pause. Did Connor actually believe in all this hocus-pocus? Earlier, he'd mocked me for saying I'd seen the 'wed-eyed monster'. Now he can smell the devil? I wanted to shout, to tell everyone, to embarrass him like he'd embarrassed me.

"The Devil?" I scoffed, despite the sudden trickle of goosebumps that ran down my neck. "*Really?*"

"It's true," said Connor, stamping a foot. "T-R-O-O-O. Everyone knows the devil smells like eggs."

I rolled my eyes.

Nazirah leaned in towards us. "That may actually be true. I once read a religious textbook, which claimed that the devil is supposed to smell of rotten eggs."

I shuddered. She'd *read a textbook*!

Connor fixed his pleading eyes on Michael. "You believe me, don't you, mate?"

I winced. I didn't like Connor calling Michael his '*mate*'. I didn't like it at all. Michael was *my* mate, not his.

Zach, the makeup-wearing activity leader, then continued his spooky tale, keeping the torch beneath his chin. "Glenkilly has a deep, dark secret," he began. "This land… these woods… are… *haunted*."

Someone howled in fear and a charge of terror ran through my veins. Was it true about the devil? Was *that* the creature I'd seen in the woods?

I'd hoped this trip would make me a bit braver, being away from home and trying new things. Mr Hopton had said that *'challenging experiences can bring out the best in people'*, which was odd for him to say because whenever challenging things happened at school, he panicked.

Though, in all fairness, when everything at school was calm and well-organised, he panicked then too. In fact, if you told Mr Hopton that the price of bus fares in Outer-Mongolia had increased by one pence, he'd probably panic about that as well.

Still, Mum's words were etched on my mind. "When you try something new and scary, that alone is being brave," she'd said as she cleaned the toilet, which I thought was pretty brave in itself.

"But what if I get frightened?" I asked.

Mum smiled at that. "You probably *will* be frightened of doing some things. But if you go ahead and do them anyway, that's being brave."

I wasn't convinced. And I certainly hadn't felt brave at all since we'd arrived at Glenkilly, with the dead animals and the red-eyed monster and Hamish's neon-bright teeth. And this voyage into the black forest, which was supposedly haunted, was making matters far worse.

Like me, Mr Hopton didn't seem happy about the situation. "Now, now," he said, with a quiver in his voice, "I think it's about time we went back to –"

"The ground beneath us is possessed by something evil," Zach went on, clearly in his element. "There are demon forces at work here and this river is their passage into the land of the living."

Mr Hopton tried to interrupt again. "I'm not sure that this is appropria–"

"And I am going to prove to you that something dangerous and otherworldly is present here tonight. I'm going to show you that this land is… *cursed!*"

Zach crouched by the river, moving his hands towards the water.

"This is *sooooo* lame," Imogen complained, loud enough for everyone to hear. *The Girly, Whirly, Twirly Gang* all snickered in agreement – though their anxious eyes told a different story.

"Shut up, Imogen!" growled Connor, before muttering beneath his breath. "God, I hate her."

We waited a while longer as Zach busied himself by the water's edge.

"What's he even doing?" Michael asked.

I shrugged. "Dunno. Maybe he's trying to catch a fish with his bare hands."

"I've done that before," Michael answered. "Remember when I caught that trout?"

"No," I said. "You found a dead trout by the canal and then picked it up. That's not the same."

It was only then that I noticed Michael's bag. For some reason, he was wearing his huge red rucksack on his back, which looked seriously heavy. In the shadows, the bag reminded me of massive snail shell and I imagined Michael as a mutated superhero. Half snail, half human. Okay, I admit it, a pretty useless superhero.

"Why do you have that bag?" I asked, as we waited by the riverbank.

Michael grinned. "Got to be prepared. I learned that in the Ghanaian Army."

I nodded. Michael had never been in the Ghanaian Army, mainly due to the fact that he was only ten years old. But also because he left Ghana when he was still a baby.

"So what's in it?" I asked, nodding at the bulky rucksack.

"Oh… erm… sunflower seeds."

I narrowed my eyes. "Sunflower seeds? You've got that massive bag, just for some seeds? Why would you even need sunflower seeds?"

"I told you, Jeremy. You have to be prepared."

"For what? An afternoon of gardening?"

Michael shook his head. "I've got other things in here too."

"Like what?"

"Erm…"

He removed the rucksack and rooted through it, listing the bag's contents. Distracted, however, I was no longer listening. I was focusing on Mr Hopton as he stepped towards the water where Zach was busy with some unseen task.

"Listen, young man, I think we should be getting back to camp now. These stories are going to give the children nightm–"

He didn't get chance to finish his sentence because, at that very second, something so astonishing happened to the river that I refused to believe my eyes.

CHAPTER EIGHT: UTTER CHAOS

An explosion of bright flames danced above the river, licking at the sky like hungry orange tongues. It was a terrifying sight! The water had erupted into a wild blaze – hot enough to roast a Christmas turkey – and our class had erupted into a wild frenzy.

"Something evil is coming!"

"It's the devil!"

"RUUUUUUUN!!!!!"

There were screams!

There was panic!

There was utter chaos!

And that was just Mr Hopton.

People bolted in all directions, stampeding through the trees, trying to find their way back to camp. Buster's booming bark echoed through the woods like a Hound of Hell. Unsure where to go, I panicked, my chest rising and falling in sharp jerks.

"This way!" wailed Mr Hopton.

We followed the sound of his bleating voice, torches beaming in every direction. Low branches swatted our faces as we raced through the trees, squeals and shrieks piercing the cold air.

Fear stabbed at my throat and I could barely catch my breath. By the time we stumbled across our campsite again, my heart was thrashing like an eel in a goldfish bowl.

Everyone quickly gathered. Mr Hopton counted us three, four, maybe five times and was eventually satisfied that we'd all made our way back to camp. Breathless panic filled the air, despite Mrs Dodd's reassurances that everything was going to be okay. Some people cried for their mummies, while others wanted to go home.

What had caused that huge blaze on the river? How could running water set alight? Was Zach telling the truth about the curse and the demons using the river as a passage? Was this somehow related to the *thing* I'd seen in the woods?

With us all huddled together, I felt a lot safer. We shone our torches on the nearby trees, expecting some sort of demon to come rushing out – but nothing stirred.

Mr Hopton marched over to Zach.

"What on Earth was that little trick all about?" he hissed. "These children are ten years old! Do you think that scaring them to death is funny?"

"Hey, I'm sorry," said Zach, holding up his hands in surrender. "It's just a silly story. We didn't expect them to get spooked like that."

"We always tell that tale of the Glenkilly Curse," said Kat, the moon reflecting on her glasses. "The kids usually like it."

"Poppycock!" Mr Hopton huffed, before pointing a finger in Zach's face. "I shall be making a formal complaint about this."

"It makes you wonder," Mrs Dodd wisely added.

Zach's fearful eyes flashed to Kat, who lowered her head, staring guiltily at the floor. They skulked away from our teacher like a pair of naughty teenagers.

"It happened again," Zach grumbled.

Kat muttered something in response but, frustratingly, I didn't quite catch the words.

CHAPTER NINE:
ICICLES OF SNOT

For the rest of the night, a sense of dread hung over the campsite like a dark, heavy rain cloud. We were so far from the normal world now, so cut off and alone.

The temperature had seriously dropped and puffs of steam danced with my every breath. After changing into my Chewbacca onesie, ready for bed, I was still freezing so put on my coat too.

I crossed the lawn towards the toilet block, which was a small brick building, like a depressing, windowless bungalow. It had a door for the boys and a door for the girls and two tiny vents that let in hardly any fresh air, keeping the bathrooms stagnant and stinky, just like the toilets at school.

As I approached, I heard whimpering about demons and monsters, which made it even harder to forget about everything that had happened. And then I spotted Connor... acting *very* suspiciously. He checked over both shoulders before disappearing down the side of the toilet block.

What was he up to?

I couldn't help but spy.

Creeping to the end of the brick building, I peered around the corner. A row of sinks ran along the outside of the toilet block, where campers could clean their dishes after a meal, and right there, in the deepest shadows, stood two dark figures – one tall, one much shorter – and although I couldn't see their faces in the gloom, I recognised both voices.

"But you promised," whined Connor.

"I'm sorry," said Zach. "We can't... not tonight. Patience, little cuz. We have a whole week." Zach placed a hand on his cousin's shoulder. "You saw how everyone reacted to the fire. Your teacher will be alert tonight. We have to be very careful now."

Connor stamped his foot. "What about the abandoned farm?"

"I'll show you the farm... eventually. Just not tonight. I have someone to deal with tonight."

What the heck were they talking about?

Why did they have to be '*careful*'?

Where was this '*abandoned farm*'?

And who did Zach have to '*deal with*'?

My nerves tightened. I had to get away from here before they knew I'd been listening. Being around Connor made me feel uncomfortable, scared even. And the more I saw of him and his cousin, the less I trusted them. I couldn't shake the feeling that they had something *sinister* planned.

Once I'd washed my face and brushed my teeth, I headed back to the tent. The panic from the blazing river had died down. Mrs Dodd was patrolling the area, ushering everyone into their tents, and apart from shuffling feet and whispering children, all was now quiet.

As I squeezed into my sleeping bag, I kept my coat on. My nose felt like an ice cube and I imagined it running in the night, icicles of snot forming at my nostrils.

"So," said Michael, "do you think it's real? You think this place really is haunted?"

"Something weird is definitely going on," I answered with a tremble in my voice.

Annoyingly, Connor was sharing a tent with us. "Well, I won at archery," he boomed. "Nothing weird about that."

I ignored him. "Could the fire on the river be related to that *thing* I saw? And the rabbits? And the badger?"

Daniel Henshaw

"You're an idiot, Jellyfish. Zach's just telling stories. And you didn't see nothing in the woods. That was just you and your stupid imagination. You're so childish."

"I am a child." I glanced nervously at Connor, now wrapped up in his sleeping bag. "So, if the whole thing is fake, how did Zach start the fire?"

Connor's mouth twitched as he swept his black fringe from his eyes. "Well… you see… Zach, erm… well, Zach didn't exactly tell me *that*. But he will do. Tomorrow."

Connor's words about the devil smelling like eggs came back to me. He was all bravado now but he seemed to believe… *something*.

I wanted to ask about the 'abandoned farm' but I couldn't. If Connor knew I'd been spying on him, he'd kill me. He'd probably take me out into the woods and tie me to a tree, until that red-eyed beast returned.

Shivering, I couldn't bear the cold any longer, so I ducked into my sleeping bag, covering my head and wrapping up tight.

"Night, Michael," I called out from the depths of my nest.

"Night, mate," he replied.

"Night, Jellyfish," said Connor.

I winced.

Then Connor turned to Michael. "Night, mate."

I double-winced.

"And you better not snore, Jellyfish!"

"I know *I* don't snore," said Michael. "That's a guaranteed fact."

I didn't respond... but a few minutes later, Michael was snoring like an asthmatic bulldog.

Closing my eyes, I tried to forget about the red-eyed monster and the dead animals and the fact that I was in a dark field, near a dark forest, with no lights and no mum and nothing but a thin sheet of fabric to protect me from all the dangers of the outside world. And with that tornado of troubles twirling through my brain, I thought I'd never be able to switch off.

But soon enough, the long day caught up with me. A warm glow hugged my whole body, the whispers of the wind melted away and I drifted off into a peaceful sleep.

Until I heard the scream.

CHAPTER TEN: SWEDISH CAVE-WOMAN

I don't know how long I'd been asleep for when a piercing shriek jolted me awake.

Where was I? Not at home. Not even in a bed. Why was I in a sleeping bag? Of course. The camping trip. Glenkilly Castle.

Both eyelids blinked open and my ears tuned into the eerie stillness. Other than the gasps of Michael's snoring and the leaves rustling in the breeze, I heard no other sound… just a cold, ghostly silence.

Had I *really* heard a scream? Or had I dreamt it? I waited for a while, refusing to shift. Even the tiniest movement would risk allowing cold air into my sleeping bag's cosy oven.

I listened again.

Nothing. Nobody made a fuss. Nobody was outside, looking for a damsel in distress.

I must have dreamt it. What had I even been dreaming about? I couldn't remember.

Then a sound made me hold my breath.

Crunch… crunch… crunch…

Footsteps.

Someone, or something, was moving around outside.

I poked my nose out of the sleeping bag.

The footsteps came closer.

Crunch… crunch… crunch…

Who could it be?

The antlered creature I'd seen in the woods?

Demons from the river?

A man in a kilt?

Crunch, crunch, crunch.

Closer and closer.

And then…

"AAAAAAAAHHHHH!!!"

Another scream! Loud and real.

My heart pounded so hard, I could feel it in my throat. Sickness churned in my stomach. I looked across the tent to see Michael, one white eye staring back at me.

"Did you hear that?" I asked.

"Yep," he replied, both eyes now open.

Then I glanced at Connor's sleeping bag. Flat, shrivelled and empty, like a deflated balloon.

"Where's –?"

I didn't get chance to finish.

"AAAAAAAAHHHHH!!!"

More screams.

Footsteps pounded the grass outside.

Panting breath.

Grown-up voices.

Mr Hopton.

Mrs Dodd.

"It makes you wonder," I heard her mutter.

I finally stood up, the night chill instantly hitting my bones, before nervously creeping to the entrance.

Zzzziiiiiippp!

Poking my head out of the tent, I peered across the campsite. Our tents had been arranged into a horse-shoe shape, with an open area of grass in the middle and the toilet block at one end. People were now buzzing across the grass with torches flashing in all directions, like a frenzy of frantic fireflies. There were squeals and shrieks, wildly waving arms, and fingers pointing nervously at the trees.

What the heck was going on?

From our tent, I could see that everyone was awake now. They emerged awkwardly through zipped entrances – as though their tents were strange beasts giving birth to them. Children gathered anxiously on the grass in a variety of colourful onesies; Spiderman, Pikachu and at least three unicorns. It was like a midnight meeting of the world's most popular film characters. Except they weren't characters… they were our classmates. And judging by their nervous yelps, they were scared.

As my eyes swept across the strange scene of shivering children, anxious adults and flickering flashlights, I still saw no sign of Connor. I glanced back at his sleeping back, double-checking it was empty. Where on Earth could he be? Was he the one who'd screamed? Surely not. Perhaps he'd made someone else scream. Yes, that was far more likely.

"Who's making all that noise?" Michael asked from his sleeping bag, his voice croaky.

"Not sure," I said. "Looks like *The Girly Gang.*"

"They had an argument or something? Probably used Imogen's make-up without asking."

I snorted a laugh but knew it wasn't true. Whatever had happened, it looked and sounded serious. Curiosity finally got the better of me. "I'm going to find out."

Michael jumped to his feet. "Wait for me."

We struggled to fully open the stiff zip before stumbling onto the wet grass, the damp ground squelching between our toes. Frosty air nipped at my nose and my breath made little clouds before vanishing into the dark sky, where the moon hid behind black clouds. Torch beams continued to flash here and there and everyone's eyes were wide and alert as they crowded around Mr Hopton near the toilets.

A dim light bulb, glowing above one of the toilet doors, had attracted a gang of mischievous moths. I eyed the insects cautiously as we crept closer.

Next to the sinks on the outside of the toilet block, stood Imogen with her best friend, Yasmine Kumar, tears drenching their cheeks as they huddled together.

"We're not making it up!" Imogen wailed at Mr Hopton.

Her usually straight, blonde hair was now frizzy and wild, like a Swedish cave-woman. Her voice – normally sneering and pompous – was broken and raw with emotion.

"It was standing right there!" she screeched, her shaky finger pointing away from the tents, towards the edge of the woods. As one, we all turned to look. Torch beams lit up the nearest trees, but beyond that we could see very little, just shadows… as though the forest within was a deep black hole.

People whimpered and shrieked and Mrs Dodd tried her best to soothe them by singing a song.

"*If you're happy and you know it, clap your hands!*"

Mr Hopton scowled. "This is not the time for singing!" he snapped, before turning back to Imogen and Yasmine. "You're scaring everybody, girls. This better not be a joke."

"Do we look like we're joking?" barked Yasmine.

They didn't. Even in the darkness, I saw that their eyes were bloodshot. Their hair was tangled and snot dripped from their noses. They definitely weren't joking. I'd seen stand-up comedians in the past and they never looked like this when they told jokes.

"Okay," Mr Hopton bleated. "Go through it, step-by-step. Tell us exactly what happened."

With her coat-sleeve, Imogen wiped the snot from her upper lip, her ladylike image long forgotten. She sniffled before

speaking. "W-we came t-to the t-toilet and… it was all fine…
until… until… we stepped out here again… and, and…"

"And *what?*" Mr Hopton was losing his patience.

"And… it was j-just standing there… with… with these great
b-big antlers coming out of its ch-cheeks." She sniffed. "It was
horrid, like a huge b-bear – but with these awful antlers… and
glowing red eyes."

An icy shiver brushed over my skin.

Antlers?

Red eyes?

The same thing I'd seen.

My mind flashed to the river of flames and Connor's mention
of the devil and Zach's tale of demons from the underworld.

And I began to wonder… just how much danger were we
really in?

CHAPTER ELEVEN: ALL. MADE. UP.

Seconds later, Zach appeared. Too quickly, I thought. The walk from the castle to our campsite took at least five minutes. How had he arrived so fast? Had he already been nearby? If so, why? And where the heck was Connor?

"Hey guys," Zach breathed with his soft voice. "What's going on?"

"We saw a monster!" Imogen wailed.

Someone shrieked at the word. Others murmured. Even the moths on the light above the toilet door appeared to scatter in fright. Mrs Dodd was still whispering. *"If you're happy and you know it, clap your hands!"* Nobody clapped. The whole class huddled together, as though being closer would make us safe.

Zach, strangely, didn't appear to react at the news of a monster sighting. No shock, no surprise.

"Now, that may not be true," said Mr Hopton, trying to keep everyone calm, though clearly agitated himself.

As I turned to look at the crowd of worried faces, all ghostly in the pale torchlight, I heard a familiar voice.

"What's happening here?" said Connor, now standing with Zach. Where had he been? It seemed like a major coincidence that he'd appeared moments after Zach. Why hadn't he been in the tent before? Something smelt off, and not just the toilet block.

Stepping aside from the huddled crowd, I moved towards Connor. He swept the black fringe from his eyes, inspecting me with disgust.

"What do you want, Jellyfish?"

I hesitated before speaking. "Where were you?"

Connor scowled. "What's it got to do with you?"

I shrugged. "Nothing. Just asking."

"I've been to the toilet, if you must know."

"What for?"

Connor huffed. "I'll give you a clue. It was brown and sticky… and it wasn't a stick." He snorted a laugh, glancing up at his cousin for approval – but Zach didn't smile; he was still watching the crowd.

Seconds of silence passed before I next spoke.

"Imogen says they saw a monster. The same one I saw."

"The monster isn't real, Jellyfish!" Connor snapped. Again, he looked up at his cousin. They shared a moment of awkward eye-contact, silently communicating... and although I had no idea what was being said, my guts churned with worry.

Teary-eyed, Imogen repeated how they'd been to the toilet before finding the creature by the trees. "It had antlers and red eyes," she whimpered.

"Just like the one I saw." Everyone turned to look my way, frowning and fearful. Connor tutted.

"Enough!" Mr Hopton shrieked. "I'm sick of hearing this ridiculous story about a monster. You're scaring everybody." He turned to face us all. "In fact, you're all scaring each other with these silly tales. It stops right now. Do you know how stressful it is to bring a classful of children camping? Let me tell you... very! So the last thing we need is for you lot to start making up stories about monsters."

"It's not made up!" Imogen yelled.

"Enough! I don't want to hear another thing about a monster or a beast or a creature. Whatever you saw, it was nothing like that. It was just a stag or a squirrel or something."

"A squirrel?" I said.

"This is some sort of… *mass hysteria*," our teacher announced, ignoring me. "I've heard about these cases where one person in a crowd faints and then they all drop like flies. That's what's going on here. One of you thinks you've seen something, so now you all do."

"I haven't seen anything," said Connor, "because it's… All. Made. Up."

"Precisely," Mr Hopton agreed. "Nice to hear you say something sensible for once, Connor."

Imogen and Yasmine huddled closer to their friends, their teeth chattering. I wondered what would happen now. Would we just go back to our tents? I couldn't imagine getting any sleep after all this excitement. The air filled with murmurs and grumbles and whimpers and whispers, and one emotion could be heard clearly in everyone's voice: fear.

The camp manager, Hamish, then arrived. His eyes looked panicked, though there were no creases across his tanned forehead and I wondered if he'd had Botox injected into his face to get rid of the wrinkles. He was carrying a large torch but didn't have it turned on. I guess his teeth were bright enough for that job.

"What's going on, guys?" he asked.

"This is all *his* fault!" Mr Hopton suddenly snapped, pointing at Zach. "He's the one who said this place was haunted. He's the one who mentioned demons and evil spirits. He's the one who set the river on fire. And look what's happened now!"

Hamish stared at Zach, open-mouthed like a confused toad. "Demons?"

"It's just the Glenkilly Curse," said Zach, anxiously fiddling with the leather strap around his wrist. "We always tell that story."

"It's not Zach's fault," said Connor, stepping towards Mr Hopton. "He just told a stupid story. It's not his fault if idiots like Jeremy are thick enough to believe it and then think they've seen something in the woods."

I felt my face redden again.

"Enough!" snapped Mr Hopton. "I don't want to hear anything else about curses or ghosts or ghouls. In fact, if I hear anyone else mention this monster, I'm going to ring the coach company and ask them to pick us up immediately. Got that?"

Everyone, including Hamish and Zach, lowered their eyes to the ground, nodding in agreement.

I, meanwhile, was thinking about what Mr Hopton had said before – that it was all just mass hysteria. It could've been a reasonable explanation. Zach tells us about the passage for demons and the river bursts into flames, then we all start seeing those demons. It would've made sense... except for one minor detail... I saw the creature *before* we even met Zach.

CHAPTER TWELVE:
TOO TENSE FOR TENTS

We were gathered by the toilet block, quietly shivering in our pyjamas and colourful onesies. Shaky hands held torches, their lights beaming mostly at the ground. No one spoke. The atmosphere was so tense, you could cut it with a moderately sharp butter knife. Nobody wanted to go back to their tents. It was too tense for tents.

"Why can't we sleep in the castle?" Imogen asked. "There's nobody else staying here, is there?"

Scratching the back of his neck, Hamish looked unsure. "Well, no, there are no other guests. But, the thing is, the castle is really struggling for money at the minute and you only booked to use the camping facilities."

"Poppycock!" Mr Hopton interrupted. "We're staying in the castle for the rest of the week. And that's that! You can't expect our children to stay out here at night after your staff members have scared them half to death."

Zach tried to speak. "Well, I only –"

"I demand that you re-accommodate us to the castle – or I shall be making a formal complaint. And not only that, I shall go to the newspapers and the TV stations – local, national, global – and I will inform them of how you have mentally scarred our children, practically ruining their lives."

"Yeah," Michael wisely added.

Everyone gave Mr Hopton a round of applause for his speech while Hamish shifted awkwardly on the spot. For once, his car-salesman charm appeared to have deserted him. He fiddled with his diamond earring before nodding.

"Okay guys," he said. "Gather your things. I'll sort some rooms for you."

*

Unlike the ground floor of Glenkilly Castle – where there were huge paintings on the walls, fancy leather chairs sitting proudly in each room and expensive-looking ornaments on every surface – the upper floor was far less classy. Depressing brown carpets ran down plain, narrow corridors with simple white doors on each side. Our bare bedrooms had creaky beds with thin, moth-eaten sheets. And the electrics were so bad that when you turned on the light, the room seemed to get darker!

Still, it was warmer than being outside. And now, safely inside a solid brick building, those dangerous woods felt far, far away.

Again, Michael and I were stuck with Connor, who seemed over the moon about being indoors. As we lay in bed with the dim light still on, I wondered if this was all part of Connor and Zach's plan… to scare everyone so we'd get moved inside. I certainly couldn't shake my suspicion that the cousins were up to something. Snippets of the conversation I'd heard kept returning to me.

We have to be careful now.

Abandoned farm.

I have someone to deal with.

Though I couldn't make any sense of it yet, it sounded very fishy. Plus, Connor had been out of the tent when I'd heard the screams. What had he been doing? And how did Zach arrive so quickly on the scene? There had to be some kind of link between them and the creature.

I thought of Zach, the black-haired goth – with his piercings and tattoos and dark makeup. He looked like he'd walked straight out of a Grimm fairytale; the kind of villain who'd chop off Rapunzel's hair without a second thought before throwing it in a cauldron full of rat tails and newts. Was he somehow conjuring the monster with a spell? Could he actually *be* the monster?

I pulled the thin white sheet over my head and tried to shake these thoughts away. My imagination had gone into turbo mode. *Zach turning into a monster?* Ridiculous! Connor was probably just happy because he was *inside* the house, closer to his big cousin, his hero. After all, he couldn't stop talking about him.

"Zach's room is downstairs," he said from the bed opposite mine. "Number five in the staff corridor. He said I can chill in there tomorrow. Watch a film. A horror film. An eighteen!"

Michael nodded, impressed. "I've seen loads of eighteens. I saw a zombie film that was so scary, it had a 'Twenty-Eight' certificate."

Perched on the end of his bed, Michael was sorting through an assortment of items in his big red rucksack. I could see a random selection of objects spilling from the bag: a torch, a Swiss Army Knife, a set of bolt cutters, twenty-seven pence in loose change, a pair of pyjama bottoms, a cigarette lighter, three Pokémon cards, a packet of sunflower seeds, two thimbles, a three-inch piece of string and a voucher for a half-priced Big Mac.

I was about to ask how Pokémon cards could possibly help in a life-or-death situation when the bedroom door suddenly opened and Zach himself slipped into the room like a silent shadow, before sitting on Connor's bed. With his thin, pale face and the dark make-up around his eyes, he looked just like a skeleton... a skeleton with long hair and green clothes on.

Connor fizzed with excitement. "Did you change your mind? Are we going out?"

Zach shook his head. "I still have something to sort out. I just came to see if you guys are okay?"

Connor nodded, grinning a demonic grin. "I'm so glad the Glenkilly Curse story spooked those idiots. It's so much better in here. Lovely and warm."

Yanking the thin sheet away from my face, I looked over to Connor's bed.

"Hang on," I said. "Glenkilly Curse? What curse? We don't know *anything* about the curse. You never told us the story."

Michael agreed. "Yeah. You just mentioned some demons and then the river set on fire."

Zach smiled. "Okay. You want to hear the story of the curse?"

Connor turned on his baby voice. "Are you sure you're not gonna cwy, Jellyfish?"

I wriggled in my bed. "Well, um, it *is* late. Maybe we should get some sleep and save the story for tomorrow."

"Shut up!" Connor snapped. "Zach is telling the story right now and you're going to listen."

"I'm not scared," said Michael. "I've seen a 'Twenty-Eight' certificate zombie film."

"Well, this isn't about zombies," said Zach. "And, unlike your movie, this story is real."

"R-E-E-E-L!" said Connor. "Real."

Getting comfy on Connor's bed, Zach shuffled his bottom, rubbed his hands in glee and then began telling us the tale of the Glenkilly Curse.

CHAPTER THIRTEEN: THE GLENKILLY CURSE

"Many years ago, there lived a rich, powerful duke."

Zach was in his element, sitting in our gloomy bedroom, recounting the tale of the Glenkilly Curse. He sat on the end of Connor's bed, hunched like an old witch over a cauldron.

"What's a duke?" Michael asked from the bed next to mine.

"It's a bit like a prince, mate," said Connor.

I winced. *Mate?* Michael was *not* his mate!

"The duke was very rich and very handsome," said Zach, still wearing his green Glenkilly uniform. "In fact, he was so good-looking that he married the most beautiful lady in Scotland. The duke owned almost all of the Glenkilly area. The woods, the fields. He owned two castles and almost everyone who lived here worked for him. But still, he was not happy."

"Why not?" I asked. "Sounds like he had a good life."

"Well, Jellyfish, if you'd stop interrupting, Zach might be able to get on with the story."

Zach smirked before continuing. "When the duke married his beautiful bride, he wanted to give her a gift. And although he already owned two castles, the duke desired another for his new wife. He demanded that one be built in her honour."

Michael gasped. "And that's why Glenkilly Castle was built!"

"Let's not rush ahead," said Zach, a devilish smile hopping onto his face. "There's a lot more to this story. There was only one part of Glenkilly that the duke didn't own and that was the area where the castle now stands. At that time, the land was occupied by a small highland tribe, or 'clan', as they were known. The clan had a tiny village of simple wooden huts. They owned a few animals, collected fruit from the trees and fetched water from the river. The duke decided that he wanted *this* land for his new castle, so he sent the commander of his army on horseback, with a dozen armoured troops. The commander demanded that the clan move on – or the duke would send an entire army to get rid of them. Being such a small clan, terrified of the consequences, the clan's leader promised to move his people peacefully. But only on one condition."

Here, Zach put on a strong Scottish accent, imitating the clan leader.

"*We have a burial ground in the centre of our village. This is a sacred place where the spirits of our dead are at peace. Once we have gone, you may do as you like with the land, but please do not disturb the deceased. For, if you do, this place will be forever haunted – by a creature so vile you'd never imagine it in your worst nightmares.*"

I felt the hairs stand up on my neck.

"What did the duke do?" Michael asked.

"Well, after the commander of the army reported back with this warning, the duke burst into laughter. He wasn't worried about the threats of a tiny hillside clan. He was the Duke of Glenkilly. Throughout his life, things had always gone his way. He owned all of the lands around, he was married to the most beautiful woman in Scotland, he had more riches than he could spend. No, he would not worry about the clan's pathetic warning. He would build a castle wherever he liked. And this would be the new home for his darling wife."

"So he built Glenkilly Castle on top of a graveyard?" asked Michael. "What about the curse?"

"Well," said Zach. "The Glenkilly Curse. Now that's where this story gets interesting."

He was about to go on when the door suddenly opened and Mr Hopton burst into the room.

"Right, lights out then. You've got a very busy –" He stopped when he saw Zach. "What are *you* doing in here?"

"Just saying goodnight to my cousin. I'll be off now."

Mr Hopton glared after Zach as he left the room, shaking his head. He then told us to be quiet, turned out the light and pulled the door closed, leaving us in pitch blackness. I wondered if Connor might continue the story from where Zach left off – but he didn't. Moments later, I heard Michael snoring and, before I knew it, the long day caught up with me once more and my heavy eyelids slammed shut.

TUESDAY

CHAPTER FOURTEEN: FRANK I.C.G.

After Tuesday's breakfast, we visited 'The Games Room' on the castle's third floor. Here, we found an ancient arcade machine, a board game with half the pieces missing and a pool table that leaned ever-so-slightly, causing all the balls to roll to one corner.

A massive window filled an entire wall and light poured in, picking up the thousands of dust particles that danced through the air. Michael and I wandered over to look out. Brooding clouds filled the sky, heavy with rain and danger. The surrounding woodland was mostly dark pine trees with the odd splash of Autumn's red and yellow. Knowing that the antlered creature was hidden somewhere within those trees gave me the willies.

Silently noting that Michael hadn't complained about his 'Window Allergy', I watched a black crow soar gracefully above the forest, searching for a spot to roost… and then something strange caught my eye.

In the distance, the scaffolded tower – that we'd noticed on arrival – loomed above the trees, menacing and oddly out of place. From the ground, the tower had appeared to be surrounded by dense forest. But now, from the third floor of the castle, I had a clearer view.

The tower stood at the fringe of a vast clearing, near a filthy-looking pond with rubbish floating on the surface and a strange cloud of gas hanging above it. A series of cylinder-shaped buildings were potted around the clearing and hundreds of bulldozed trees were scattered around the water's edge, like corpses at the end of a violent battle.

What was that place? It looked like they were making a real mess of the countryside.

A waft of flowery perfume then hit my nostrils and I turned to see Kat standing next to us.

"Hi guys," she said, her voice a soft Scottish squeak. Her hair was almost as orange as Hamish's skin and a cute row of freckles ran across her button nose. She was quite pretty in a strange sort of way.

"What's that?" asked Michael, pointing into the distance. "Looks like the Eiffel Tower or something."

Kat smiled uneasily. "Erm… well… the land over there belongs to our neighbours. The company is called *Frank International Conservation Group,* or *Frank I.C.G.* for short. They look after the local wildlife."

I glared back at the disgusting scene. Had Kat lost her mind? Why would a conservation site contain a filthy, litter-filled pond with a cloud of gas hovering above it? Why would a conservation site knock down those beautiful trees?

"But what's that tower?" I asked.

"Oh…" said Kat. "That's the Lookout Tower. It helps their team to see for miles, so they have a better view of the animals below and the birds in the sky."

"Lookout Tower?" I said.

Kat nodded. "Yeah… and if you see an eagle coming, you turn to your friend and shout… 'LOOK OUT!'"

Michael chuckled.

"He gets it," said Kat, grinning.

But now I was worrying about eagles and whether they were strong enough to grab a skinny ten-year-old.

Before I had chance to ask this, Kat changed the subject. "So, are you boys looking forward to the Go-Karts this morning?"

I heard Michael claim that he'd driven a Formula One car in the past – but my mind had drifted. When I turned away from the window, I spotted my arch-nemesis, Connor McCafferty, being led out of the Games Room by his cousin, Zach. As they left the room, Connor glanced around nervously, his head twitching like a meerkat. What were they doing? I couldn't let this opportunity pass, so I left Michael chatting to Kat and followed them.

Creeping to the exit, I waited by the open door. Soundless as a shadow and hidden from sight, I listened to the cousins in the hallway.

"It'll definitely be tonight," said Zach.

Then, just as I strained to hear more clearly, I realised I was being watched. Opposite me, near the door on a small chair, sat a girl named Leah Ford. Wearing thick specs and her hair in pigtails, she stared at me like a puzzled goldfish, her mouth wide-open. Lifting a finger to my mouth, I silently shushed her before she had chance to speak. Her brow knitted, like a toddler eating an olive for the first time. I moved my ear closer to the door.

"Of course they won't catch us," Zach was saying. "It's orienteering tonight. You'll be free to wander about. That's when we'll go."

"To the abandoned farm?" asked Connor.

"Yes. But first, we'll go back to the river."

The *abandoned farm* again! What were they plotting? I was straining to listen once more when Leah's voice made me jump.

"What are you doing, Jeremy?" she boomed with no volume control whatsoever.

The conversation in the hallway stopped so I didn't hang around. Darting across the room, I squeezed between Michael and Kat, nodding as if I knew precisely what they were talking about.

When I glanced back at the door, Connor had reappeared, his eyes searching the room from behind his black fringe. Had he heard my name? Did he know I'd been listening? I tried not to make eye-contact. But luckily, I'd heard enough. Tonight I would take action. Tonight I would find out what was *really* going on at Glenkilly Castle.

CHAPTER FIFTEEN: SLOW AND STEADY WINS NOTHING

Apparently, there's nothing like whizzing around a race track at three-thousand miles-per-hour to help people forget about a red-eyed killer monster. Not that I'd be forgetting anytime soon.

We'd followed Kat into the woods, staring warily into every dark shadow, expecting something to be watching us. But as Mr Hopton had banned any talk of the creature, no one dared say a word.

After a short walk, we arrived at an opening, where a small Go-Kart track snaked its way through the overgrown grass and six rusty Go-Karts were lined up on the start line. A crumbling storage unit stood by the track, which must have been where they kept the Go-Karts overnight.

Once the races began, I stood next to Michael, watching the Go-Karts zoom by. I wanted to tell him what I'd heard earlier between Connor and Zach, but Connor – annoyingly – stayed by Michael's side like an unwanted shadow.

"Okay, next six," said Kat, guiding the previous racers away from the course. They stepped off the track, giggling and cheering. I couldn't understand why they were so happy; they'd spent the last ten minutes risking their lives, driving what looked like tin-openers on wheels.

I was part of the next group, leaving Michael and Connor together by the fence. I sighed, hesitating, but I had no choice. Mr Hopton shoved me onto the track.

"Don't forget to tighten your helmets," he bleated, constantly wringing his hands. "And remember to brake."

The helmet's chin-strap pinched my skin. When Kat came to check my seatbelt, I tried to tell her but she flicked on the engine and its chainsaw-buzz drowned out my timid voice. The Go-Kart vibrated violently like a second-hand washing machine, almost bouncing me out of the hard seat.

When Kat waved the flag to go, every engine roared and the other Go-Karts flew off down the track.

Mine didn't.

Not trusting these fragile machines, I refused to risk my life by driving like a maniac.

Slow and steady wins the race.

I'd heard someone say that once.

As my vehicle inched away from the start line, I glanced around to see some people pointing, sniggering behind cupped hands.

And then I saw Michael.

He wasn't laughing at me. He wasn't even looking at me. Michael was listening to something Connor was saying… and then he *did* laugh, heartily, at one of Connor's jokes. Connor, grinning like a wolf on the verge of a kill, slapped him on the back as though they were best mates.

I felt a part of my heart crack.

And then Leah Ford lapped me.

After our ten minutes were up – and I'd been lapped by everyone (many times) – I came to the conclusion that the old saying was a load of codswallop.

Slow and steady wins nothing.

Retaking my spot at the fence, I watched Michael and Connor strap themselves into their Go-Karts, before noticing I was alone.

Behind me, with no interest in the racing whatsoever, stood *The Girly, Whirly, Twirly Gang*, speaking in hushed whispers, possibly about the previous night.

No one had believed *me* when I'd first spotted the antlered-creature in the woods. Everyone had mocked me. But now two of the most popular girls in school had seen it too. We had something in common. We could join forces. My reputation could finally be dragged from the gutter.

I was about to say something inspirational – something that the girls could relate to, something that would cause them to pull me into their inner-circle – when Yasmine Kumar turned to face me. Thin as a pencil, Yasmine had a sneering face with pursed, lemon-sucking lips and a wrinkled nose, as if she were constantly about to sneeze.

"Go away, Jeremy."

My mouth opened stupidly for moment, unsure what to say.

"Did you not hear me? I said, go away."

The rest of the gang were looking now, frowning and disgusted, as though Yasmine were cleaning dog muck off her over-priced designer trainers. Their eyes seemed to look right through me.

Some jellyfish are transparent.

"I just wanted to talk to you and Imogen," I said, glancing around to see Mr Hopton still focused on the race. I lowered my voice anyway. "About the… *creature*."

"Well, we don't want to talk to you."

"But we saw the same thing," I said, almost pleading with them.

Imogen suddenly spoke, tucking a strand of blonde hair behind her ear. "You have no idea what we went through, Jeremy. You weren't even there."

"But I saw the monster in the woods, remember? Everyone laughed at me but… we saw the same thing."

Someone snorted.

"You're just trying to copy us," said Imogen. "You're just jumping on the bandwagon."

"What? No, I saw it *before* you, remember? In the afternoon."

Imogen shook her head, eyeing me with pity. "You're so fake, Jeremy. Everyone can see through you. Connor's right. You're just a jellyfish."

As one, the gang then turned away from me and continued talking in voices so hushed I couldn't hear a word they were saying.

What was Imogen talking about? I knew precisely what I'd seen in the woods: the same creature as them. One way or another, I had to prove it. I had to prove it to Mr Hopton, to those stupid girls, to Connor, to Michael and, most importantly, to myself.

The Go-Karting session had been a disaster. I'd finished last, Michael had spent the whole time laughing and joking with Connor, and now the only people who'd also seen the beast were totally rejecting me.

There was absolutely no way that things could get any worse.

Then Kat made an announcement.

"And the winner is… Connor!"

Great.

CHAPTER SIXTEEN: TRESPASSERS WILL BE SHOT!!!

"Each group has a different starting point," Hamish announced, holding up a clipboard.

Wrapped up warm for the evening, we were gathered outside the castle, next to a huge monkey puzzle tree. Millions of stars glistened in the night sky and an old-fashioned lamp-post lit the area – though I'm sure Hamish's teeth could've done the job.

"When you get to your starting point, guys, you'll find a clue. Solving the clue will tell you your next location. You all have maps, guys. Use them to navigate your way around the grounds."

This caused a few whimpers.

Hamish immediately switched to calming mode. "Don't panic, guys. The grounds are well-lit. And none of the clues are near the woods. Everything will be fine."

"And make sure you're wearing sensible footwear," Mr Hopton quickly added. "It may not be raining but the grass will still be squelchy. And don't forget about the dangers out here; the breeze, the moths, the twigs."

"And the wed-eyed monster," Connor sneered.

Someone laughed at this. Someone else sobbed.

Hamish held up his clipboard. "The first team back here – with all the clues solved – will be the winner! Good luck!"

With that, most groups raced off to their starting points while *The Girly, Whirly, Twirly Gang* linked arms and moved slowly, staying close to Mrs Dodd. Our group – Michael, Connor and me – followed Zach. Connor held our clipboard, which had a map and an answer sheet clipped to it.

"What's our first location?" Michael asked. "I won gold at the Olympics for Orienteering."

"Who cares?" said Zach, glaring at us through a layer of black eyeshadow. He snatched the clipboard from Connor before shoving it into Michael's hands. "You two can crack on with this. We've got something we need to… *attend* to."

Connor smirked before strutting off towards the gloomy forest with his cousin. Michael gave me a confused glance so I filled him in about the conversation I'd overheard this morning and their plans to visit the '*Abandoned Farm*'.

Michael's frown deepened as he listened. "So, are we following them?" he asked, a small shake in his voice. He was wearing his bulky red rucksack, containing his torch, sunflower seeds, cigarette lighter and a whole load of other useless things. "Into the woods?"

I shook my head. "No. We're not going into the woods. Not yet."

Spinning back towards the castle, I saw that everyone had gone now. The adults wandered about the grounds, keeping their eyes on the children, who were all searching for clues. The castle's huge oak doors stood wide open, with no one keeping guard. This was our chance.

Pulling Michael by the arm, I dashed past the monkey puzzle tree, constantly checking we hadn't been spotted, and darted directly for the big door.

"Where are we going?" asked Michael.

I didn't answer.

Inside the castle, a warm fire crackled away to the left of a staircase with a varnished wooden banister, beautifully carved into delicate patterns. The building smelled fusty, like an old museum, and a noisy clock tick-tocked away down the corridor. More paintings of frowning men hung on the walls as well as another stuffed stag's head. The sight of the antlers made me shudder.

Without hesitating, I raced to the staircase.

"Where are we going?" Michael asked again.

"It's up here," I said, taking the stairs two at a time.

"*What's* up here?" Michael panted, keeping up.

At the top of the stairs, I turned to a door on the left.

NO ENTRY

STAFF ONLY

TRESPASSERS WILL BE SHOT!!!

(with a water pistol)

After checking no one was around, I turned the handle.

Michael gasped. "What are you doing?"

"Everyone mocked me, just because I saw something in the woods. I need to know the truth about this place."

"But why are we going in here?"

"To look for clues… in Zach's bedroom."

"Clues? You're not Sherlock Holmes, Jeremy. I mean, you couldn't even cope with Cub Scouts or football training or that time I asked you to make me a sandwich. I don't think we should be poking our noses into any of this business. Monsters, curses... goths."

My shoulders slumped. "You're right. Things are getting pretty dark... and I guess I'm just a stupid jellyfish. But you know what?"

I straightened, puffing out my chest.

"Jellyfish can glow in the dark."

CHAPTER SEVENTEEN: POT NOODLES AND STALE SWEAT

I had no idea what might be on the other side of the door. But I had to show Michael that I wasn't scared. I had to show him that Connor and Zach couldn't be trusted. So, biting down my fears, I pushed open the door and stepped through. Michael followed. Along a narrow corridor, we passed a number of doors.

MANAGER'S OFFICE

LAUNDRY

DRYING ROOM

The gloomy passageway smelled of Pot Noodles and stale sweat. Was this really where the staff spent their free time?

Eventually, we came to a numbered door.

ROOM 01

Pipes rattled and clunked behind the walls as the central heating laboured into action. We passed more doors.

ROOM 02
ROOM 03
ROOM 04

I thought back to Connor's words last night.

Zach's room is downstairs.

Number five in the staff corridor.

And here we were.

ROOM 05

Luckily, it wasn't locked. Groaning inwards, the door opened into Zach's dark lair. I flicked a switch on the wall and a light above flickered into action.

My eyes were first drawn to Zach's desk. An army of unlit candles littered the workspace, streams of dried wax dripping down their sides. In amongst them, Zach had a plant pot shaped like a human skull, a snow globe with a tombstone inside and a crucifix statue with skeleton attached. Aggressive jewellery lay strewn across the window sill, alongside pots of black nail varnish.

"What are you even looking for?" asked Michael.

I ran a finger across the desk, making a trail through the dust. "Clues."

On a nearby shelf, lined up like crumbling soldiers, stood a row of ancient books. *Frankenstein* by Mary Shelley, *The Strange Case of Dr Jekyll & Mr Hyde* by Robert Louis Stevenson, *Scottish Myths & Legends* by Rosemary Gray. Books on black magic and witchcraft.

I'd not read the novels but I knew the stories. Dr Jekyll, a gentle man, drinks a sinister serum and becomes the evil Mr Hyde. Dr Frankenstein collects dead body parts and brings them back to life... as a monster.

"Looks like he's into crazy doctors," I said.

Michael didn't answer, his eyes still darting nervously about the dark room.

"Maybe he has a split-personality like Dr Jekyll," I whispered. "Maybe he drinks a potion and turns himself into the monster."

Michael didn't answer.

"Or maybe he's bringing dead things back to life, like Frankenstein. Those dead rabbits, perhaps. Maybe –"

Finally, Michael did answer. "Maybe you're over-thinking this, Jez. He's a goth. He likes creepy books. That's it."

"Hmmm."

Next to the books stood a row of DVDs. Horror movies. *The Fly, An American Werewolf in London, Cinderella.* On his bedside table were two black, wooden photo-frames, decorated with tiny skulls around the edges. There was a picture of Connor in one, smiling like butter wouldn't melt on his evil tongue, and a photo of a black-haired woman in the other. I guessed it was Zach's mum... as the word MUM had been carved into the frame.

The goth's room was pretty weird, with his creepy ornaments and his strange jewellery... and then I noticed his bed. Horror of horrors... a Peppa Pig quilt cover. I almost threw up.

"We shouldn't be here," said Michael. "Let's go."

I shook my head. Apart from the obvious weirdness, I hadn't found anything suspicious... yet. I pulled open a drawer next to his bed. A random assortment. Sunglasses, a ruler, pin-badges with more skulls on them. Pens, foreign coins, playing cards. I opened the drawer below. Socks... black socks. I slammed it shut with a *BANG*.

"Shhh…" said Michael. "We'll get caught if you keep making all this noise."

"There has to be something that proves he's involved with the creature."

The bottom drawer scraped open. Boxer shorts, all black except for one yellow pair with Spongebob Squarepants on them. I was about to push it closed when I noticed something at the bottom of the drawer. Sticking out from beneath the pants. A passport. I grabbed it.

"Maybe he has a secret identity," I said, flicking through the pages.

"We should go," said Michael, joining me by the bedside table. "I've done these kinds of searches with the police before… and you need a warrant."

Ignoring him, I found the page with Zach's photo and his personal details. Could Connor's cousin really be a secret doctor, working with black magic in the Scottish wilderness to conjure a mythical beast?

No. Well, not according to his passport.

Surname/Nom (1)

McCAFFERTY

Given Names/Prénoms (2)

ZACHARY WILBERFORCE

Michael snorted. "Wilberforce?"

Putting the passport back beneath the boxers, I couldn't help but giggle. I shut the drawer and stood up. "I guess that explains why he's so odd."

Michael laughed before giving me an Elbow-Bump. A warm rush ran through my veins. It felt great to have Michael back by my side, instead of seeing him joking around with Connor.

Michael nodded towards the door. *Time to go.*

"One more minute," I said, stepping over to a wardrobe. Inside, clothes hung on hangers. Only two green Glenkilly uniforms broke up the line of black shirts.

Michael stood next to me, looking in. Two boxes sat at the bottom of the wardrobe. One had the word *OUIJA* printed on top, the other had nothing.

"What's Oo-ja?" asked Michael.

"No idea," I said, lifting the lid. Inside was a board. I unfolded it to see the board had the letters of the alphabet on it.

"You know what this means?" said Michael.

I raised an eyebrow but didn't answer.

Michael snorted. "He doesn't even know his ABC."

Unimpressed, I put the board away and replaced the lid.

Next, I opened the plain box.

And when I looked inside, I could not believe my eyes.

We'd finally struck gold.

CHAPTER EIGHTEEN: MISSING CHILDREN

I knew immediately that we'd found treasure.

At the bottom of Zach's wardrobe sat two boxes. One, labelled *OUIJA,* contained a basic board game to help him learn the alphabet. The other – a plain black box – was filled with newspapers. *Jackpot!* The top newspaper was dated the previous month and as I read the article, my insides began to flutter.

The Inverteine Record

BEAST IS BACK!

Report by Poppy Peat

Police were called out to Glenkilly Castle once again yesterday, following reports of a **missing child**.

At approximately 3pm, the Inverteine Force received a call, informing them that a child had vanished from one of the school parties camping within the grounds.

According to staff, a young girl (aged 10) disappeared in the middle of the night. After discovering she was gone, the Glenkilly workforce searched the grounds but saw no sign of her.

Castle manager, Hamish Quinlan (45), spoke to us late last night. "At 9am, we were told that a girl walked off in the night. Staff here knew she'd be safe as there is no way out of the grounds without access to the gate controls. However, after a prolonged search, we saw no sign of the girl. At that point, we informed the police."

The castle, Glenkilly's most popular tourist attraction, is now an activity centre for children, specialising in outdoor and adventure sports. However, this isn't the castle's first incident of this nature. *The Inverteine Record* has previously reported on **four occasions** when a child has gone missing at the campsite **this year** – and Sergeant Mary Hooley feels extremely disappointed by the whole situation.

"This type of incident should not be occurring – especially so frequently – at a location as popular and respectable as Glenkilly Castle. The constant calls about missing children have already caused terrible damage to the reputation of both the castle *and* the local area."

Fortunately, the young girl was found minutes before the police arrived. Again, Sergeant Hooley was not impressed.

"To arrive on the scene, *once again*, and be told that there is no longer a problem, is extremely frustrating. Of course, we are pleased that the child is now safe but we are a small force and an hour's round-trip to Glenkilly Castle is a waste of precious time. Inverteine has a huge teenager problem at the minute – with alcohol and graffiti and littering – so we can't really afford to waste our time. Glenkilly Castle needs to tighten up security measures to ensure that all of the children are safe and this type of incident does not happen again."

Castle manager, Mr Quinlan, responded to this by saying, "When people are camping, there's not a lot we can do if they decide to wander off in the middle of the night."

The child was found in the woods by activity leader, Zachary McCafferty (21), who also spoke to us. "The girl says she was chased through the woods by something that looked like a bear." Similar to previous incidents, the child claimed that the animal had antlers or huge tusks coming from its face and bright red eyes.

The constant sightings of this animal, now known locally as 'The Glenkilly Beast' – as well as the high number of 'missing children' calls to the police – has seen the castle take a huge financial hit, with many schools demanding refunds, almost all of October's bookings being cancelled and hardly any reservations made for the winter months.

The castle has already suffered financial difficulties in recent years, with the owner – Lord Forster of Stirling – having to sell off many acres of his land to a conservation company. This most recent episode will be another big blow to the local community.

Thankfully, the child is now safe and well. Her parents have been informed of the incident and the school has reluctantly agreed to go ahead with the rest of their camping trip.

In other news, a large number of dead frogs have been found floating on the surface of the water near…

I almost dropped the newspaper. My hands were shaking.

"I don't believe it," I said.

"I know," Michael breathed. "Hamish's surname is Quinlan."

I flicked through the other newspapers. They all reported sightings of the antlered-creature and children going missing in the night.

Headlines shouted things like:

COPS CASTLE CALL
ANOTHER MISSING CHILD!
CASTLE IN CRISIS!

Panicked thoughts rattled through my head.

- An ongoing epidemic of missing children, quickly found, just before the police arrive.
- Sightings of the beast, the thing *I'd* seen.
- Mentions of Hamish and Zach, who obviously knew about this stuff – but had played dumb when *I* saw the creature *and* when the girls did.
- Problems with the police.
- Constant references to the castle's financial troubles.

- And why was there no mention of 'The Glenkilly Curse', the story that Connor and his cousin apparently knew?

Zach had these newspaper articles stuffed into a box at the bottom of his wardrobe. Why? This was the clue I'd been looking for... but I had no idea what it meant. Was Zach behind it all? Was he controlling the beast? Chasing children so they'd run off in the night? And if so, why?

I didn't have the answers.

But I knew it meant... *something.*

CHAPTER NINETEEN: SEVEN DEAD FROGS

I felt sure that Zach was up to something dodgy. We'd seen plenty of evidence in his bedroom: the books about crazy doctors, the newspaper articles, the Cinderella DVD. And I knew precisely where the cousins had gone – a place we'd been before.

When we stepped outside, groups were still buzzing around the castle grounds – clutching their clipboards as they tried to solve clues – but Michael and I marched straight past them. We had our own clues to solve.

Glenkilly was draped in shadows and, as we moved away from the castle, the darkness grew deeper.

"Where are we going now?" said Michael.

"You'll see," I answered, trying to sound brave. But as the woods drew closer, my nerves tightened. Still, I had to find out what Connor and Zach were doing. I had to catch them at it. I had to show Michael that I wasn't a wimp.

Michael pulled the torch from his rucksack and turned it on. Our breath made clouds of warm mist as shadows shifted and twisted in the torch's beam. Every time I heard something move, I expected the antlered beast to come rushing towards us. I thought about turning back for the castle but I knew that Connor was out here, and if Connor – with his silly black fringe – could face this then so could I.

First, we'll go back to the river.

Those were Zach's words outside the Games Room this morning. So that's where we headed. The quiet whisper of its current gradually grew into an angry roar as we moved closer. We paused by the riverbank, expecting to see the cousins here. But neither was in sight.

Creeping cautiously, careful not to snap the twigs beneath our feet, we moved to the water's edge. The river slithered past menacingly, hissing and fizzing. Just yesterday, we'd seen this snaking body of water flare into a great ball of flames. Now, above it, hung a thick curtain of fog. We could barely see the opposite bank of the river... as if the fog were hiding something on the other side.

Strange. There'd been no fog in the rest of the forest. Just here, above the water. Zach had talked about this place being a passage to another world. I shivered, staring nervously at the mist hovering around us. Could it contain a demon? Something evil? A ghost?

Michael and I huddled closer. With all this creepiness and rumours of curses, the least we could do was stick together. We had to be strong and brave and sensible.

And then one of us broke wind.

"Urrgghhh!" I groaned. "Was that you? Smells like rotten eggs."

"More like cabbage soup," said Michael, covering his nose.

"Melted Stilton," I added. "You could've warned me!"

"I didn't do it," Michael protested.

"Well, neither did I!"

Then I remembered the smell from the night before. Connor had called it the 'Smell of the Devil' and even Nazirah had agreed with him. I shuddered, wondering if there might be something otherworldly here with us, and a trickle of goosebumps slithered over my skin.

Only then did we spot the dead frogs. Seven dead frogs, scattered by the river bank, as though the water hadn't liked the taste and had simply spat them out.

"Poor things," said Michael.

We stood in silence for a moment, staring at the fog and the frogs, listening to sounds of the forest and the river.

And then I noticed something.

"Listen," I said. "Listen to the water."

Michael cocked his ear at the river.

"That doesn't sound right," he agreed.

Carefully, cautiously, we moved to the water's edge, peering into the river as Michael shone his torch onto the inky surface.

Crouching by the riverbank, I strained my eyes before spotting something rather odd. "What are they?"

"Bubbles," said Michael. "The water is bubbling from below."

As I leaned closer to the water, I could now make out thousands – if not millions – of bubbles, fizzing furiously in the water.

"Where are they coming from?" I asked. "Should a river even *be* bubbling?"

"Well," said Michael, "I can make bubbles like that… in the bath."

I snorted a laugh before Elbow-Bumping him.

"Seriously, though," I said, "I've never seen a river do this. Then again, I've never known a river smell so bad either."

A howling, hateful wind then scraped its invisible fingers through the trees, shaking the branches above us... and then Michael's torch flickered.

Once. Twice.

On, off. On, off. On.

Before... the torch failed completely, plunging us into total darkness.

My chest tightened. With everything cloaked in black, I could actually *feel* the weight of the darkness around us, like some vile creature with huge black wings, threatening to grab us and squeeze us until we could no longer breathe.

"Turn it back on," I yelled.

"It's the battery," said Michael.

"Well, put a new one in!"

"I don't have any *batteries*!"

"Not even in your enormous bag?"

Michael shook his head.

"But you have Pokémon cards and a load of sunflower seeds? Really useful when we can't see! *'Be prepared for all situations.'* That's what you said earlier."

"Hang on," he growled, removing the rucksack and then bending down to search through it. He rummaged around before

118

pulling something out. I heard a sharp flick and saw a quick spark of light. A cigarette lighter. He flicked it twice more, sparking a couple of times, before eventually getting the result he'd wanted.

With Michael bent down, right by the river bank, a small yellow flame appeared on the top of the lighter. But the little flame lasted only a second because, just like the previous night, the river suddenly burst into an enormous orange inferno, hot and angry.

At first, the flames frightened me. Was some evil force at work here? Was some despicable beast about to rise from another dimension?

But then I came to my senses.

The fire on the river had nothing to do with the devil or the underworld. Michael had started it with his mum's lighter. And there was nothing special about the lighter. It even had a *Poundland* sticker on it.

So, what did this mean? *Anyone* could set the river alight… which meant that Zach had done just the same yesterday, which meant that Zach was playing a big trick on everyone. But why?

Questions pinballed around my brain with no answers in sight. However, there was one thing I now knew for certain… Zach was up to something very dodgy.

CHAPTER TWENTY:
THE ABANDONED FARM

A gate squealed in protest as Michael pushed it open and we stepped onto a stony lane. On one side of the path, stood three crumbling stone bungalows. On the other, a big cattle shed with walls of corrugated iron that shook noisily in the wind, banging like a big metal drum. In the centre of the lane, an old-fashioned lamp-post gave off a dim glow.

"What is this place?" Michael asked, flashing his torch at the cowshed.

"A farm," I replied. "I heard Connor and Zach talking about it this morning."

Once the river fire had died down – and no demons or ghouls had appeared – we'd headed deeper into the woods. Chased by ever-darkening shadows, we'd trekked through acres of squelchy woodland, before stumbling across the dishevelled farm buildings.

"But it's empty," said Michael. "Where are the animals?"

The cold voice I heard next chilled my blood.

"Dead," said Zach. We turned to see him standing by one of the bungalows, Connor next to him.

"Sorry?" My voice came out shaky.

"Dead," he repeated. "Or gone."

"What do you mean?" I asked.

Zach stepped into the middle of the stony lane. "The answer to your question. The animals are dead. And the ones that survived were taken away. Before the farmer abandoned it, this farm was owned by Lord Forster, the owner of Glenkilly Castle."

"Why are you two here?" Connor growled. "You're meant to be orienteering."

"So are you," I said.

"As far as the story goes," Zach went on, ignoring his cousin, "something went *very* wrong with the animals; they became sick, scarily thin. Then they started acting strangely; sheep head-butting walls, goats rolling around on their backs for hours, chickens laying the tiniest eggs. And finally, fur and feathers falling out in great chunks."

My mind flashed to Buster: bald patches on his back. The dead rabbits near the archery: tufts of fur missing. The dead badger, the frogs.

Zach continued. "The farmer thought something was wrong with the water so he asked the conservation company next door, *Frank I.C.G.*, to run tests on the river. They agreed but said the water was fine. *Frank I.C.G.* blamed it all on the telephone lines. The farmer complained to the phone company. But they said he was talking rubbish. Yet the animals got worse. So the farmer left, taking the surviving animals with him, and the farm's been empty ever since."

It sounded strange. Telephone lines causing animals to get sick. Did that really happen?

I expected Zach to then tell us another gruesome tale when he announced, "I'm going for a wee." He gave his torch to Connor before marching around the corner, instantly swallowed by shadows.

The three of us huddled beneath the dim glow of the old-fashioned lamp-post, the icy wind chilling me to the bone and bashing at the iron cowshed.

"So, were you spying on us or something?" Connor asked.

"Or something," I answered, shuddering at the cold. "What are you even doing?"

He flashed me a glare before grunting.

"Tell us what's going on, Connor. We've just been at the river. We set fire to it ourselves. There was a weird mist and bubbles and that awful stink."

"And neither of us had trumped," Michael added.

"Just tell us, Connor, does Zach know how to make the creature appear?"

Connor snorted. "Of course not. The creature isn't real. They're just stories." He lowered his voice, glancing nervously towards the spot where Zach had disappeared. "Even if my cousin believes in it, none of it's true."

I felt my nerves twang. Zach *believed* in the monster? Did this mean he *was* behind it? Even if Connor didn't know? Or was Connor just playing dumb? Denying his involvement at all costs?

Connor spoke in a hushed voice. "Zach says that finding this monster is his destiny. Ever since he was little, Zach says he's had a strong connection to the spirit world. Now he has the chance to finally capture something from another dimension. To *prove* its existence."

"So, Zach thinks it's real," said Michael. "But you don't?"

"Or are you just pretending not to?" I asked.

"Shut up!" Connor snapped.

"No, Connor. I won't shut up. I'm sick to death of –"

Connor slapped his palm across my mouth, raising a finger on the other hand.

"Shut up and listen," he whispered.

Our eyes darted around as we waited in silence.

And then we heard it.

CHAPTER TWENTY-ONE: MAKING POPCORN

Something was inside one of the crumbling farmhouses.

A frantic knocking noise echoed through the cold night. Not like the deep boom of the wind, banging the iron cowsheds. This new sound was a sharper, quicker, more meaningful rattle.

"It could be Zach," Connor whispered, urgently moving towards the stone bungalow, towards the sound. "He might be trapped."

We followed.

"It could be the creature," said Michael.

"*What?*" I gasped. "No! Come back. Let's wait for Zach."

"It's *not* the creature," Connor hissed, glancing at Michael. "Come on, mate. I'll protect you."

He then placed his arm around Michael's shoulders, causing a rocket of rage to explode inside me. I wanted to yell at him to get his hands off of my best friend – but then the sound came again. A frenzied rattling noise inside one of the ramshackle buildings. Fear gripped every nerve in my body. My words choked in my throat and my breathing became shallow.

Michael and Connor shone their torches towards the decrepit farmhouse, nervously edging closer.

"Zach?" Connor called, his voice echoing.

Silence followed.

We paused for a moment before stepping inside.

As soon as I entered, I felt another presence in the building; something… not human. Even on this cold October night, the temperature inside the bungalow seemed to have dropped ten degrees. My nose felt like it might fall off. Michael and Connor huddled together ahead of me… too close to each other for my liking. The faint yellow glow of their torches barely lit the place, instantly devoured by hungry black shadows.

"Zach?" Connor repeated, echoing once more.

Again, no reply.

The building appeared to be empty. No signs of human life. From what I could tell, the floor was covered in straw and animal droppings. The bare stone walls dripped with damp. And then my heart turned to ice as the rattling started again.

Ticka-ticka-tick. Ticka-ticka-tick.

A tiny, frantic knocking noise.

Connor waved his torch manically around the darkness but we could see very little. Just shadows and floor and walls.

"Let's get out of here," Michael whispered. "It smells worse than the boys' toilets at school."

"Don't panic, mate," said Connor. "We just need to find Zach. If he's hurt, we could save him. We could be heroes."

"N-not if the creature k-kills us f-first," I answered.

"There is no creature," said Connor, trying his best to sound brave.

Ticka-ticka-tick. Ticka-ticka-tick.

My chest tightened. Moisture dripped from the ceiling. Our breaths clouded the icy air. Connor stepped forward. We followed, as if glued to the torchlight.

And then we saw it. The source of the knocking.

On the floor amongst the straw, sat an old microwave, its door rattling as if it might explode at any moment.

"Looks like someone's making popcorn," said Michael.

"It must be broken," I said, "if the door's shaking like that."

"But who's using it?" asked Michael. "I didn't think anyone lived here anymore."

Connor moved the torchlight along the cable at the back of the microwave… which then revealed something shocking. The microwave wasn't even plugged in.

Connor gasped. "I think… I think… there's something inside it."

The rattling suddenly became fiercer.

TICKA-TICKA-TICK! TICKA-TICKA-TICK!

"Oh no!" yelped Michael. "It's the beast!"

I wanted to tell him that it couldn't be the beast. The antlered creature I'd seen in the woods was almost six-feet-tall. It couldn't possibly fit inside a standard kitchen microwave… unless Zach was somehow conjuring it up with an electrical cooking appliance.

I wanted to say all of that. But I didn't. In the pitch-black, with the dripping walls and the icy air, I couldn't think straight.

"We should go," I whimpered.

I was about to turn for the exit, and drag the other two with me, when both Connor and Michael squealed.

And the microwave door burst open.

CHAPTER TWENTY-TWO: CLINGING ON FOR DEAR LIFE

I'd like to think at a moment of such high drama, when a mythical creature may have attacked me and my best friend, that I would have done something heroic, like a spinning roundhouse kick, or a flying head-butt, or offered it some money to go away.

But I didn't.

I just stood on one leg (not sure why), pulled a stupid face and put my hands up to my chin like a gerbil cleaning itself.

And then I watched as a creature smashed its way out of the microwave… but it wasn't the Glenkilly Beast… it was a mangy old cat (that looked like it had already used eight of its nine lives).

The cat paused in front of us, glaring as if to say: *Why didn't you bother helping me?* Even in the poor light, I noticed the furless, bald patches on its back. The cat appeared to shake its little head in disgust before flopping down, bending itself in two and licking the fur around its bottom. *Gross!*

I suddenly felt silly. Terrified of a dirty, little cat that had been stupid enough to get trapped inside a microwave. I was about to laugh-out-loud when I glanced at Michael and Connor… and a small part of my heart cracked.

Michael, my best friend on the entire planet, was clinging on for dear life to Connor, my worst enemy. They were practically hugging, protecting each other from whatever may have escaped the microwave.

Why hadn't Michael held onto me? Why hadn't he tried to protect me, his best friend? *Was* I even his best friend anymore? I wanted to cry. And for the first time tonight, it hadn't been through fear of the darkness and the woods. It was through fear of losing my best friend. My only friend.

Connor's cackle, so loud in contrast to the eerie silence, echoed off the wet walls. "HAHAHAAA! That was hilarious! Stupid cat! Come on, let's go and tell Zach."

Tears formed at the corner of my eyes as I watched Michael follow Connor out of the building. He never even looked my way.

Once we returned to the stone path and the lamp-post's yellow light, Connor immediately marched off again, towards the cattle shed, towards the shadows where Zach had vanished. Michael followed.

"Where are you going?" I asked, my voice jittery.

"We need to find Zach."

I watched them continue towards the darkness.

"Michael?"

My best friend looked back. "Come on, Jez. We'll find Zach and then go."

The cat incident had put me on edge. "I'll just wait here."

I nodded at the lamp-post as if its faint glow offered some sort of holy protection. I hoped Michael would get the hint and come back. Instead, he looked at me with pitying eyes before disappearing into the shadows with Connor.

My heart sank and two days' worth of worries flashed through my mind.

Why did no one believe that I'd seen the red-eyed beast?

Was I becoming obsessive?

Was that why Michael had befriended Connor?

Or was I still acting like too much of a scaredy-cat?

After all, if Michael felt safe with me, he would've stayed here and not gone off with Connor... wouldn't he?

I knew I hadn't imagined the antlered thing in the woods. I'd seen it, alright. Just like Imogen and Yasmine – and all of those children in Zach's newspaper reports. Why on Earth did he have those articles? He had to be involved. Why else would he keep them?

The cowshed's iron walls rattled and a cold wind whipped through the lane, bringing tears to my eyes. I wiped them away before staring hard into the darkness.

Where had they got to?

I glanced at my Casio watch. It was getting late. Mr Hopton would soon be worrying about us. Whether they found Zach or not, it was time to go.

As I tapped my foot impatiently, more images of our time in Scotland raced through my head. The dead rabbits with missing fur. The bald patches on the dog, Buster, and on the microwave cat. The dead frogs. The badger. The fog above the river and the mist above the filthy pond nextdoor. The strange tower and the fallen trees. A conservation site? Really? Then there was the fire on the river and the cousins' shifty behaviour and Connor's tale about the castle being built on a burial ground. And, of course, the creature in the woods. But what did it all mean?

Something rustled nearby, snapping me from my thoughts. Someone was stepping through the bushes.

"Hello?" my high-pitched voice echoed around the deserted farmyard.

Nobody answered.

"Michael? Did you find him?"

No response.

I stared into the black shadows, to where my classmates had followed Zach… but the darkness was so deep it swallowed everything.

"Connor? Zach? Are… are you there?"

Nothing.

I listened intently… and above the breeze, I thought I could hear… breathing.

"Michael?"

I strained my neck, cupping my ear at the darkness.

An odd sound.

A wet, clicking noise, from deep within a throat.

A thin, barely-audible growl.

My nerves tightened.

"Who's there?"

Then the smell hit me. Exotic flowers, like scented candles. I'd smelled it near the dead rabbits and… hadn't I smelled it somewhere else too?

Oh no!

Focusing on the shadows, I could now make out a tall figure.

"Z-Z-Zach?" My voice was fragile.

I knew that the shape was too big to be Zach and a twang of dread strummed in my gut. Less than twenty metres away, the figure stood like a human but with something sticking out of its massive head. Antlers. Clouds of wet breath escaped its mouth and as it stepped slowly into the light, I saw saliva dripping from its knife-like teeth. Brown and hairy, like a huge, antlered bear, the creature glared… with glowing red eyes.

CHAPTER TWENTY-THREE: BROWN BREAD

Someone screamed! A shrieking voice I didn't recognise until I realised the horrid noise was coming from… my own throat!

I'd never felt fear like it; a real terror churning deep within me, causing my whole body to shake.

Closing my eyes, I tapped my feet together three times and said, "There's no place like home. There's no place like home." Just like Dorothy did in *The Wizard of Oz* before she was magically transported back to Kansas. And, unbelievably, when I opened my eyes again, much to my utter shock and amazement… I was still by the lamp-post in Glenkilly. *Damn!*

Seeing those red eyes in the darkness once more, I span and ran, acting on instinct alone. I jumped over the farm gate like a wannabe hurdler, landing with a thud. Freezing air ripped through my lungs as I blundered into the dark forest, trying not to trip on logs or slip in the mud. Thorns clawed at my legs. Branches slapped my face. Adrenaline carried me faster than I thought possible. I stumbled twice before losing my footing, banging my knee against a rock. The pain was dull and hardly registered. As I pushed myself to my feet, my hands squelched in the mud. Glancing back, I saw no sign of the beast... but I could hear something crashing through the undergrowth.

It was coming.

Sprinting off again, I almost slipped straight away. The pitch-black forest offered no light whatsoever. I only had a rough idea where to go. I heard the river hissing and headed towards it. Behind me: clumping, heavy footsteps. I didn't look back.

In the darkness, I could barely see and almost ran straight into the river. As I peered into the black trees, wondering which way to turn, my legs suddenly felt heavy. I wasn't used to this sort of exercise; a light jog for me normally required an oxygen tank and a long rest on the sofa.

Clump, clump, clump.

Heavy footsteps and horrid wet breath, heading straight for me. Red eyes glowing in the darkness. I had to move. Gambling on directions, I raced away from the river, back into the trees.

Branches flung into my face as I battled through the brush. My feet barely touched the ground. Where was Michael? And Connor? And Zach? Had the creature killed them? Had I let them walk straight into a savage attack? Or was this Zach now, chasing me after transforming into this horrid beast?

My mouth dried, my throat burned. Would I ever make it out of this black maze?

And then I saw the lights.

Like an oasis in the desert, beyond an opening in the trees, stood the castle. Using my last ounce of energy, I tried to speed up... but something suddenly dragged me back.

This was it.

The moment I died.

The moment the beast killed me.

Dead.

Brown bread.

I'd not had chance to tell Mum that I loved her one last time. I'd not had chance to become a teenager or pass my driving test. I'd not had chance to see what Marmite tasted like.

I turned, terror tight in my chest, expecting to see the monster... but no. My coat had snagged on a thorn bush. Pulling hard, I tried to tear myself away, but the large thorn had made a deep insertion into the material.

Clump, clump, clump.

Wet, panting breath approached.

I yanked harder and harder.

Clump, clump, clump!

One… last… pull.

My coat ripped away from the bush, leaving a large slash in the fabric. Mum wouldn't be happy. It was from a very, very, very, very, very expensive shop called Primark.

But I didn't have time to worry about that. Darting for the opening in the trees, I raced across the grass that led back to the castle. A sense of pure relief washed over me as I spotted the rest of our class, now gathered in front of the castle's huge oak doors. Orienteering must be over.

"AAAAAHHHHH!!!!" I yelled.

Everyone turned to look, their faces full of fear, as if a sabre-toothed tiger had just burst onto the scene, completely unaware that this was something much, much worse.

"THE MONSTER'S COMING!"

Screams erupted as the crowd began to scatter. I raced across grass, my breath deafening my ears and my heart pummelling my chest. I gave the black woods one final glance. Shadows swayed

and leaves whispered, but the creature was nowhere to be seen…
for now.

CHAPTER TWENTY-FOUR: VEIN OF DOOM

Without waiting for an explanation, Mr Hopton dragged me into the castle, away from everyone else. He pulled me into a large lounge where logs burned inside a massive fireplace and huge framed paintings lined the wood-panelled walls.

Mr Hopton plonked me down on a sofa. He remained standing, his face almost purple, with a thick vein visible in his forehead. I had a feeling he wasn't happy.

"Jeremy Green, what is your problem?"

"I have a lot of problems. Which one do you mean?"

Mr Hopton snarled. He actually *snarled*. Like a leopard with a hangover.

"This isn't funny, Jeremy! You've scared everyone to death. Again!"

"But the monster –"

"No! No, no, no! I refuse to hear anything else about this blasted monster!"

"But we were in the woods and –"

"You were in the *woods*?" Mr Hopton's eyes bulged as if they were about to pop out from their sockets. I thought the vein in his forehead might burst. "You were told not to go near the woods!"

"We followed Connor and his cousin, Zach."

Mr Hopton frowned. "*We?* Who's *we?*"

"Me and Michael."

Mr Hopton shook his head. "You were supposed to be orienteering. We trusted you all to get on with it. You lot are going to ruin our school's good reputation!"

"Our school doesn't have a good reputation," I replied without thinking.

Mr Hopton snarled again. "As for that damned Zach…" He paused, rubbing the top of his balding scalp, his forehead's vein of doom still swollen. "Wait here. And don't even think about moving."

I immediately thought about moving.

But didn't.

I watched Mr Hopton storm out of the room, slamming the door behind him, leaving me alone. The fire hissed and crackled and I suddenly felt swelteringly hot. I removed my ripped coat before wiping sweat from my face.

If only Mr Hopton would listen. I may have doubted myself before but now I *knew* the creature was real. We had to do something. Michael and Connor weren't safe out there. Mr Hopton had told me not to talk about the monster but I had to try one last time – for their sake.

The lounge door then creaked open. Mr Hopton stepped in, followed by two sheepish-looking ten-year-olds.

Connor and Michael.

Neither spoke but both tried to communicate with me. Michael gave a tiny, barely noticeable head shake, while Connor glared a death-threat. They sat alongside me on the sofa. What was going on? Why were they here? Where was Zach?

"Where is Zach?" Mr Hopton asked, as if reading my mind.

Connor shook his head. "Don't know. He went to the toilet. Not seen him since."

"Which toilet?"

"Erm, the one in the, erm, castle."

Mr Hopton huffed before looking at me and then back at Connor.

"Jeremy says that you three – and Zach – have been in the woods. Is that true?"

"No, Mr Hopton," Connor lied. "We were told not to."

Our teacher's eyes flashed to Michael.

"No, Mr Hopton," said my best friend.

A log cracked in the fire as Mr Hopton rubbed his chin.

"He also says that he saw a monster?" Mr Hopton said this as a question.

Both Michael and Connor shook their heads.

"We've been orienteering," said Connor. He held up the clipboard – the answers to the clues all filled in. My mouth opened, then closed again before I said something I'd regret.

Mr Hopton told Michael and Connor to go upstairs with everyone else and prepare for bed. Heads lowered, they trudged for the door. Connor flashed me a final warning, while Michael's frown was full of a pity I didn't want.

Once they'd gone, Mr Hopton sat next to me, his voice softened.

"Jeremy, what's going on?"

Biting my lip, I remained silent.

"Talk to me, Jeremy. This whole monster thing. It doesn't make sense. You got the girls wound up yesterday and then they had their nightmares about it."

They didn't have nightmares, I wanted to say. *They really saw it.* But I remained silent.

"And now you're getting your friends into trouble."

"Connor's not my friend."

"Okay, but tell me why you keep going on about this...
creature."

Because it's real, I wanted to say. But I knew Mr Hopton
wouldn't listen. I knew he was angry with me, despite this 'Good
Cop' routine. So instead, I told him what I thought he'd want to
hear.

"I just get scared sometimes," I whimpered. "My
imagination gets the better of me."

Mr Hopton nodded, totally buying it. "I understand, Jeremy.
Staying away from home for the first time can be very scary. But
that doesn't mean you can scare everyone else."

This time *I* nodded, pretending Mr Hopton's advice was
really sinking in.

"You mustn't go off into the woods on your own, Jeremy.
You need an adult to look after you. Someone strong and athletic.
Someone you feel safe around."

I glanced at Mr Hopton's puny arms. "Like Mrs Dodd?"

"Yes, like – No! I meant me!"

"Oh."

"The thing is, Jeremy." His voice suddenly became stern. "I have to draw the line at some point. If you mention the monster again, I'll have to send you home. I'll call your mum or the coach company and you'll be out of here. Understood?"

I nodded again, lowering my eyes to the carpet.

Mr Hopton's message was loud and clear. Now I knew precisely what I had to do; not mention the monster again… not in front of Mr Hopton anyway.

CHAPTER TWENTY-FIVE: AIN'T NO BEAST

I was barely through the bedroom door when Connor pounced.

"You stupid jellyfish! Why did you tell Hoppo that we were in the woods?"

I ignored him, pushing my way into the plain room. Connor shoved me in the back, causing me to fall face-first onto my bed.

"Answer me! Why did you tell him?"

Flipping myself over, I sat up on the edge of the bed.

"I had to tell him… because… I was being chased."

Michael and Connor exchanged a nervous glance.

"Chased?" said Michael.

"The beast," I said, as if stating the obvious. "It chased me through the woods. Didn't you see it? You must have seen it."

Michael lowered his eyes, shaking his head, not even tempted to bend the truth.

Connor practically growled. "Don't be stupid, Jellyfish! There ain't no beast in them woods. It's just a story."

"But I saw it!"

Connor huffed.

A tense silence filled the air before I spoke.

"Where's Zach?"

Connor shrugged. "Couldn't find him."

My tummy fluttered. "Hang on. So, while I was being chased, Zach was missing? At the exact same time?"

Connor slammed his fist into the frame of my bed. "No! Don't even go there!"

"But what if Zach knows how to conjure this creature? What if Zach *is* this creature?"

"I said, no! It's not true. Zach would've told me."

"Jez," said Michael. "This is crazy. Why are you still talking about hocus pocus? Zach doing spells and magic? Come on, man. That's Connor's cousin you're talking about."

I frowned. Why was Michael taking Connor's side? Michael had seen the books in Zach's room. Witchcraft, black magic, Scottish folklore. *Dr Jekyll, Frankenstein.* Michael had seen the newspaper articles about the beast. Michael had seen the Cinderella DVD.

Of course, I couldn't mention any of this now. We couldn't let Connor know we'd been in Zach's room.

Nobody understood how close I'd been to death. No one believed me about seeing the beast. I still had no idea what was actually going on. Was Zach involved? Was this creature magical? Or just a wild animal?

There was one thing I needed to ask Connor. "Do you know the rest of the story? The Glenkilly Curse?"

Connor half-shrugged. "Kind of, yeah."

"Tell us."

Connor shook his head. "It's just a silly story."

"I want to hear the end."

Connor sighed before sitting down on his own bed. "You're obsessed, Jellyfish."

"Please finish it. Where did we get to?"

"The burial ground," said Michael, still standing. "The duke was going to build the castle on the clan's burial ground."

Connor nodded. "Okay. Are you sure you want to hear this? Because, after everything that's happened, it's going to sound really weird."

"I'm sure," I said. "Please finish the story."

Connor clasped his hands together, took a deep breath and told us the ending of the Glenkilly Curse.

CHAPTER TWENTY-SIX: WENDIGO

All was quiet now – bar the low rumble of the old radiators. With our room in darkness, Connor held a torch beneath his face, just like his cousin had done by the river.

"What happened next?" Michael whispered. "If the duke built the castle on the clan's graveyard, did the curse come true?"

Connor shook his head. "No... not at first. The duke and duchess were happy, living at Glenkilly Castle, riding horses, murdering foxes and all the other stuff that rich people do. But then things changed. The duke started seeing a figure in the woods, a weird creature that looked like a bear. He thought it might actually *be* a bear – they had them in Scotland back then. But he wasn't sure. The bear-thing would be there one minute, then gone. And whenever the duke told his wife or his staff, none of them had seen a thing."

The mention of the 'bear-thing' sent goosebumps down my arms. Was this the thing that chased me? I had to admit; Connor was a pretty good story-teller.

He went on. "The duke kept seeing this creature in the shadows… before it quickly vanished. He thought he was going mad. Eventually, he stopped going to the woods, scared of the strange bear. Then he refused to leave the castle at all. But it didn't help. He began seeing it at night, through the window, watching him from the garden."

"Why didn't he just go to one of his other castles?" I asked.

"He was about to," said Connor. "But the night before they planned to leave, the duke finally came face-to-face with… the *Glenkilly Beast*!"

Michael gasped.

But Connor didn't stop. "In the middle of the night, the duke's horses started making a terrible noise in the stables. When the duke went to see what was wrong, he found the horses going crazy. Then, outside the stables… he saw this gross creature… seven-foot tall, a muscly human-like body, covered in thick brown fur. It had sharp teeth and the duke thought it *was* a bear at first. But, weirdly, this thing had enormous, spiky antlers sticking out of its cheeks – not on top of its head – out of its cheeks. The duke screamed! And then fainted."

Michael gasped again. I swallowed a hard lump down my throat. Antlers? Was this the real story? Or was Connor trying to wind me up?

"The next morning, when his servants found him, the duke told them about the beast – but nobody else had seen a thing. The horses were all fine, so everyone thought the duke had finally lost his marbles. After that, the duke and duchess left Glenkilly Castle – and never returned."

"But what about the beast?" asked Michael. "What happened afterwards?"

Connor frowned. "Zach says that the beast is still here. People have seen it. And everyone who has… says the same thing. That it's the scariest thing they've ever laid eyes on. So scary that your heart will almost stop. And this is why the beast was given the most terrifying name imaginable…"

"What?" I asked.

"Maureen."

Michael tittered. "*Maureen?* That's not scary!"

Connor scowled. "Imagine being our age and having Maureen as your name."

We all nodded.

"Yeah, actually, that does sound pretty scary," Michael admitted.

"Well, I'm not calling it Maureen," I said. "That's stupid."

"Zach says," said Connor, "that they have something similar in America. They call it the Wendigo."

"Wendigo?" Saying the word aloud seemed to lower the room's temperature. "Connor... this thing, the Wendigo... you've described the exact thing that chased me. The same thing Imogen and Yasmine described."

Connor moved the torch away so I couldn't see his facial expression.

"I didn't want to believe it," he eventually said. "I just thought it was a stupid story that Zach tells people. But last night... we were in the woods... he kept telling me these stories. I didn't want to admit it, but he started to frighten me."

Connor voice was more fragile than I'd ever heard it.

"What stories did he tell you?" I asked.

Connor flashed his torchlight into my face, blinding me. "Why do you think the castle is empty?" he asked. "Why do you think there are no other school trips here?"

"Is it because Mr Hopton is the only teacher stupid enough to book a camping trip in Scotland during October when it's freezing?"

"Well, yes, there is that. But it's not freezing *inside* the house. Zach says they usually have schools staying here all winter. This time last year, the house was filled with children. But not this year. You know why?"

Michael and I looked at each other before shrugging.

"Because of Maureen," said Connor. "Apparently, there have been so many sightings of the thing, chasing children through the woods, that they've had hundreds of complaints; schools wanting their money back. Some schools even cancelled their trip. The castle's reputation is ruined. Everyone's heard about the Glenkilly Beast – apart from Mr Hopton, apparently. And now look at the place. We're the only school here. The castle is running out of money and will soon be out of business if something doesn't change."

I wanted to tell Connor that we already knew about these stories, that we'd read about them in the newspapers in Zach's room. But I couldn't... not yet. We still didn't know Zach's true connection to this thing. Connor seemed genuinely upset and I

153

felt like I'd misjudged him. Zach, on the other hand, was still out there.

"So why does Zach keep telling the story?" I asked. "If the sightings of this Wendigo are causing people to stay away, why does he keep telling children that the place is haunted?"

Connor lowered the torch again. "I asked him the same question. But he just had one answer for me… he said that *'they'* make him tell it."

WEDNESDAY

CHAPTER TWENTY-SEVEN: THIRTEEN CRANE FLIES

October mornings in Scotland were bitterly cold. The grey skies were full of dark clouds and misery – and today was no exception. It was the kind of morning that ice cubes would've preferred to stay in bed, a morning for sitting by the fire, watching your favourite movies and drinking hot tea.

Instead, we were going to see who could float across a freezing cold lake on a thin strip of wood. Or, as Hamish called it, canoeing.

After breakfast, we followed the camp leader through an archway at the rear of the castle, which led to some sort of stable yard, though there were clearly no horses around. I wondered if this was where the Duke of Glenkilly had come face-to-face with the Wendigo all those years ago. I glanced down at the worn cobbles beneath my feet. Could I have been standing on the exact spot where the duke had fainted?

The stable yard was an open, square-shaped space with a bin (shaped like a frog) standing in one corner. The grubby windows that looked into the old stables were either cracked or missing and the green paint on stable doors was flaky and peeling.

Hamish unlocked a large door in the farthest corner of the yard, opening up a dark room, which I presume hadn't always been used for storing canoes. The door opened, releasing a big breath of cold air and dust.

"Right, guys," Hamish announced. "You'll need to collect a canoe with your partner. Then we'll take them over to the minibus and take a short drive to the lake."

Queueing in pairs, I'd partnered with Michael. Behind us, Connor stood with Nazirah. There was still no sign of Zach.

"Aren't you worried about him?" Michael asked, spinning to face Connor. "He's not still out there, is he?"

"Who?" asked Nazirah. "What's happened?"

"We're not sure," said Michael. "We think Zach may be in trouble."

"Zach's not in trouble!" Connor snapped. "He obviously knows his way back from the abandoned farm."

"Abandoned farm?" said Nazirah.

Connor ignored her. "We don't need to tell anyone about last night. Zach can look after himself. He can survive. He once went hunting and killed thirteen crane flies."

"Woooaaahh!" Michael gasped, with a look of genuine admiration in his eyes.

Nazirah snorted. "Do you even know what a crane fly is?"

"Erm, not exactly," said Connor. "But they sound dangerous. And he killed at least fifteen, maybe seventeen or more."

"The crane fly," Nazirah explained, "is the proper name for an insect more commonly known as the 'Daddy Long-Legs'. You know, those silly harmless flies with gangly legs that can't even fly straight, as if they've been drinking wine all day."

"I knew that," said Michael, seriously pouting to hide his mistake.

Connor's face hardened, glaring at Nazirah, but he didn't answer.

The line for the canoes inched forward as the first two people passed us, carrying their boat. The mud-caked canoe looked heavy and needed a person holding it at each side.

Turning back to Connor, I decided he should know the truth. "There's something we have to tell you, Connor. Yesterday, we searched Zach's bedroom."

Connor's eyes filled with poison. "You did *what?*"

I raised my palms defensively. "Try not to be mad. We know it was wrong but we found something very interesting. We think he's involved in conjuring up the Wendigo."

Connor grimaced before switching his gaze to Michael. "You too?"

"It was Jeremy's idea."

My heart sank.

Michael was throwing me under the bus!

A Connor-shaped bus!

The very worst kind of bus!

Flashes of yesterday replayed in my head. Michael and Connor laughing by the Go-Kart track. Michael and Connor holding each other when the cat jumped out of the microwave. Michael and Connor wandering off *without me* to look for Zach.

Was I being rejected? Abandoned by my best friend?

As the line shuffled forward again, Connor bit his lip so hard, I thought he might draw blood. "So, what did you find?"

"Evidence," I said, "which shows that your cousin has a special interest in the Wendigo. We think Zach is behind it all."

"*You* think that," said Michael dismissively. "*You're* the only one that thinks it's real."

Another dagger to my heart.

After everything we'd seen and everything I'd told him, Michael still refused to take my side.

"Guys," said Nazirah. "I have absolutely no idea what's going on. Did you say *Wendigo*? As in the American monster that lives in the woods and eats people?"

I nodded. "But apparently, around here she's called Maureen."

Nazirah's eyes narrowed. "Maureen?"

"It's got nothing to do with you, Nazirah," Connor snarled, baring his teeth like a wolf.

"Okay," she replied, holding up her hands in surrender. "Fair enough. But whatever you're up to, be extra careful of those *crane flies*… and the moths, and especially… woodlice!"

Connor growled but didn't respond. His eyes were wild and angry when he glared back at me. "So what *evidence* did you find?"

"He's… erm, well… he's collecting newspaper articles."

Connor snorted. "That's it? That's your evidence to prove he's involved with Maureen?"

"But all the articles are about missing children, children who all claim they've been chased by an antlered creature at Glenkilly. Zach is even mentioned in some of the newspapers."

"And? They're news reports about the place he works at. There's nothing weird about saving those. My mum still has a newspaper clipping about a lost hamster – just because she knows the woman who lost it."

I grunted. Why wasn't Michael supporting me? I suddenly felt silly again, like when I'd first seen the monster. But I was right about that, the monster *was* real. And I felt right about this too… Zach *was* involved.

As we moved forward in the queue, a crow settled on the stable roof before squawking a murderous cry. We were now close enough to see inside the storage area, which – along with canoes – was filled with clutter; old paint tins, rusting tools and bags of rubble. Dust and cobwebs had invaded every corner.

Hamish stepped past us, looking busy and important, and Connor took the opportunity to speak to him.

"Where's Zach?" he asked, putting a hand out to stop him, like a half-sized Lollipop Lady.

Hamish stopped dead in his tracks, glancing uneasily at Connor. "Zach's, um, busy," the orange-skinned man replied, before quickly darting back inside the storage room.

Hamish helped the pair ahead of us with their canoe and Michael and I moved to the front of the line. I was about to step inside the gloomy old stable, which smelled of compost and neglect, when something caught my eye on the ground nearby. Somebody had dropped a brown leather wallet next to the frog-shaped bin.

I moved away from the line and, crouching to pick it up, I instinctively opened the wallet. Inside it, an I.D. card showed a photo of the wallet's owner, alongside the person's details; their name, address and job.

I was about to snap the wallet shut – when I noticed something odd. I recognised the face in the photo but the name was different. So was the job. What the heck was going on? Why would this person have a false name? Why would they have a second job? How strange. With suspicious thoughts swirling like a sandstorm in my mind, I slid the wallet into my coat pocket before moving to rejoin the queue.

However, after seeing me distracted by the wallet, Connor had seized his opportunity and partnered up with Michael. He smirked as I watched them carry their canoe to the minibus.

CHAPTER TWENTY-EIGHT: HAVING KITTENS

Nazirah (my new partner) and I both wanted to sit at the front of the canoe. So, after a quick debate, we came to a fair compromise and Nazirah sat at the front. We learned how to paddle in a straight line. We learned how to change direction. We even learned how to turn our canoes three hundred and sixty degrees. Thankfully, being paired with someone as smart as Nazirah made everything easier.

It was all a bit much for Mr Hopton. With all the algae and the duck poo and the untold dangers hidden beneath the surface, he was having kittens whenever someone touched the water. I never understood that saying. *Having kittens,* meaning when someone panics. Why would they have kittens? I imagined Mr Hopton at school with heaps of little cats appearing under his desk anytime someone returned from the toilet without washing their hands.

The canoe then tipped a little, snapping me from my thoughts. I was amazed at how the dainty boats didn't topple over. So far, Hamish had made us do all sorts out on the water, like jumping jacks, standing on one leg, singing 'Heads, Shoulders, Knees and Toes' (with all the actions). And although the canoe rocked a bit, it never felt like we'd fall in. Which was lucky because, just like the river, the lake stank of rotten eggs.

When Hamish gave us some free time, I guided our canoe as far away from the group as possible. Coming to a stop by the bank, Nazirah said something but I didn't hear what. I was distracted, watching Michael and Connor, chatting away like best buddies. What were they saying? Was Michael blaming me for sneaking into Zach's room? Claiming that I'd forced him to do it?

It seemed like I was losing *everyone* just lately. Earlier this year, Dad had split-up with Mum. One day, he'd just emptied his wardrobe and moved in with his new girlfriend, leaving me behind like an old toy that bored him.

Before we moved into Mr Hopton's class, I had a teacher I loved, Miss Hope. Then she decided to get married and have a baby, deserting me. Even Grandad Monty – my reliable, boring old grandad – had cleared off to Thailand with his new woman, leaving me and Mum to fend for ourselves.

Nobody thought I was worth sticking with.

Apart from Michael.

But I guess he'd changed his mind.

"Jeremy!"

It was Nazirah's voice. She'd spun around in the canoe to look at me as we sat at the edge of the lake, far away from the others. "What were you guys talking about earlier?"

I shifted awkwardly. "What do you mean?"

"Don't act dumb, Jeremy. You were on about some weird things. What's happened to Connor's cousin? Where's the abandoned farm? Why were you talking about a Wendigo? And who the heck is Maureen?"

I trained my eyes on the reeds by the bank. "I'll tell you later. I want to ask you something else. Have you ever heard of this *Frank International Conservation Group*? Before we came here, I mean. Had you ever heard of them before this week?"

"*Frank I.C.G.*?" She thought for a moment before shaking her head. "No."

I nodded. Nazirah knew everything about everything. I mean, her favourite TV show was the news, for goodness sake. She even knew the capital city of a country called Panama. I didn't even know it was a place – I just thought it was a hat. And yet, she'd not heard of this strange conservation company, who knock down trees and fill their pond with litter.

"Something definitely smells off with them," I said. "Almost as eggy as this lake."

Nazirah laughed.

But as soon as the words left my mouth, an explosion of thoughts scattered through my brain:

Eggy lake. Stinky water.

Bubbles in the river. The strange mist.

Frank I.C.G.'s grounds. Mist above the dirty pond.

Dead frogs. Dead Rabbits. Dead Badger.

Cats and dogs with no fur.

The farm with the sick animals.

Frank I.C.G. ran tests and blamed the phone lines.

An idea was forming in my head, itching every part of my brain... but I couldn't quite scratch it.

"Are you okay, Jeremy?" asked Nazirah. "You've been staring at the sky with your mouth open for the last three and a half minutes."

"Sorry. I was thinking."

"Oh right. That's your thinking face, is it? I've never seen it before... and I sat with you in class for six months."

"Something's not right."

"Something's not right? Are you okay, Jeremy? Do you feel ill?"

I shook my head. "No. *Frank I.C.G.* I can't quite put my finger on it but I have a feeling the conservation group is somehow connected to the fact that this water smells like poo. I also think *Frank I.C.G.* had more to do with the abandoned farm."

Nazirah frowned, totally flummoxed. "What abandoned farm?"

I ignored the question, instantly distracting Nazirah by handing her the wallet. "Recognise that person?"

Nazirah opened the wallet and inspected the I.D. card, her brown eyes widening. Then she frowned, confused.

"But that's –"

"I know," I said. "But look. Different name. Different job."

She studied the I.D. card. "*Frank International Conservation Group*? I don't understand."

I was about to tell Nazirah about last night's events when Hamish called us all together. She gave the wallet back to me before we paddled back across the lake.

"Okay, guys," Hamish yelled, loud enough for everyone to hear. "I have a challenge for you all. I want you to swap seats with the other person in your canoe. All you have to do, guys, is stand up, step by each other and sit down again. Let's see who can do it fastest!"

Everybody stood up, ready to switch with their partner. I passed Nazirah to the left, with her on my right. Everything went perfectly. We kept our balance, rocking the boat only slightly. We were going to succeed easily... until I glanced past Nazirah at something that sent anger charging through my veins.

In the next canoe, Michael and Connor had already swapped places. And much to my horror, they celebrated by doing... an *Elbow-Bump*! How dare they! How could Michael do it with someone else? Especially Connor! The Elbow-Bump was *our* special thing!

Without thinking, I lunged to my right, yelling at them to stop. "Hey!"

But that's as far as I got.

With Nazirah and myself both at the same edge of the boat, and no weight on the opposite side to balance things out, the canoe tipped and tipped and tipped. And it didn't rock back this time. We capsized, head-first, slapping into the freezing water with an almighty SPLASH!

CHAPTER TWENTY-NINE: MR HOPTON'S MEGA QUIZ

While Nazirah and I dried out, everyone else visited the castle's gift shop, where they each spent a fortune on bendy pencils, toy dinosaurs and a heap of other tacky items completely unrelated to Glenkilly. I didn't mind missing out as I had no interest in unicorn keyrings or highlighter pens that smelled like watermelon. Plus, I wanted to apologise to Nazirah for drenching her. She said it was fine and that accidents happen. But I still felt awful because it was all my fault.

*

After a Spaghetti Bolognese dinner, we went to the Games Room for '*Mr Hopton's Mega Quiz*'. I partnered Nazirah, as I had done all day, which was actually brilliant because she was super smart, like a scientist, or a doctor, or Google Translate.

Sickness churned in my stomach when I saw Michael sitting with Connor, *again*. I couldn't stop thinking about their Elbow-Bump. Every time it popped into my mind, I felt sick. How could he just do it with someone else like that? As if it was nothing. It was meant to be our thing... our *special* thing.

"Question One," Mr Hopton bleated. "An easy one to start. Sodium Hypochlorite is more commonly known as which cleaning product?"

Everyone groaned. "How are we meant to know that?" someone shouted.

I whispered to Nazirah. "It's the stuff Superman's allergic to." But she shook her head and wrote the word *'bleach'* instead.

"Question Two," said Mr Hopton. "According to its advertising slogan, which cleaning product makes 'hands that do the dishes feel as soft as your face'?"

More groans. "Mr Hopton, are all the questions about cleaning products?"

Our teacher scowled. "No! Some of them are about Health and Safety Legislation! And there's one about Barack Obama."

Everyone grumbled until Mr Hopton spoke again.

"Who was the first African American to be elected as president of the United States?"

Anyway, Nazirah got all the questions right so we won Mr Hopton's grand prize, which was a pencil sharpener. Not one each. Just one pencil sharpener between us. I let Nazirah have it, seeing as she'd answered the questions.

*

Zach still hadn't turned up when Mr Hopton called for lights out at 22:03. I could tell that Connor was a bit worried. He kept scratching the back of his hand, pacing around the bedroom and saying things like: "I'm a bit worried." But straight after, he'd add: "Not that I need to be. Zach can take care of himself."

Getting out of bed, I stepped towards the bedroom door.

"Where you going?" Connor barked.

"Toilet," I replied, opening the door. I didn't wait for a response.

The castle lights were out now and the corridor was a windowless tunnel of darkness. All was quiet, though I could hear the odd whisper. My soft footsteps padded along the carpet as I crept towards the bathroom at the end of the passage.

The bathroom door hinges groaned as I pushed inside. A fluorescent tube of light flickered into action.

As I did my business in the metal trough, I listened to the sound of a dripping tap, wondering if the Wendigo was still out there. Was Zach really behind it? Or had the creature taken him? I shuddered, remembering how close I'd been to it.

After tightening my pyjama bottoms, I was about to wash my hands when the door suddenly burst open and Connor barged in.

"What you doing in here, Jellyfish?"

I gestured towards the trough. "A wee."

"Thought you might have been going to tell Mr Hopton about last night again."

I snorted a laugh. "Why would I do that? He doesn't believe me anyway."

"Because you're a coward. K-O-W-W-E-D."

"Takes one to know one," I replied.

"Shut up!" Connor scowled. "I don't *know* anything."

"You can say that again."

"I don't *know* anything!" he repeated.

I laughed. "Yes, I've noticed."

He stepped so close to my face that I could smell his sewage breath. "No," he said. "You're twisting my words. I do know *some* things."

I laughed again. "Just not how to spell simple words."

175

Connor's face turned a terrifying shade of scarlet. "What else were you doing in my cousin's room last night?"

"I told you this morning. We were just snooping around."

"What did you find?"

"Newspapers about the Wendigo and the missing kids. He also has books about witchcraft and black magic. And stories about crazy doctors like Frankenstein and Dr Jekyll. When you put it all together, you have to admit, it looks suspicious."

Connor snarled. "Don't be ridiculous. It's just the stuff he's into. He's a goth." A long, long pause followed. "Did… did you find anything else?"

"What do you mean?"

Connor's expression softened. "Well, I've not seen Zach for a whole day now. Did you see anything that might tell us where he is?"

Connor was worried – and he wanted *my* help. The cheek! He mocks me in front of everyone, calls me a jellyfish, tries to steal my best friend… and now he wants my help!

"Yes," I said, "we found some *really* useful information."

Connor's face brightened.

"We found out… that your cousin likes Peppa Pig *and* he doesn't know his alphabet."

Practically foaming at the mouth, Connor pulled back his fist and prepared to punch me. I flinched, bracing for the impact.

And then we heard the growling.

CHAPTER THIRTY:
CURIOSITY KILLED THE JEREMY

Connor cocked his ear towards the bathroom door, slowly lowering his fist. We stood, paralysed, frozen, listening to the deep, evil growl, coming from somewhere inside the house. We turned to the door, hesitating before nervously exiting the bathroom.

As we stepped back into the hallway, the growling continued – a deep guttural rumble coming from beyond the door at the end of the corridor, the opposite end to our bedroom. Connor began tiptoeing towards it but I grabbed his arm.

"What are you doing?" I whispered.

"Going to see what it is," he hissed.

"But what if it's Maureen?"

Connor shrugged. "If it's Maureen, we'll kill it and become heroes." He said it like killing monsters was the most normal thing in the world.

I glanced back towards our bedroom, hidden in the darkness. I should've gone straight back to bed and left the growling creature alone. But curiosity got the better of me. What was it that Mum always said? *Curiosity killed the cat.* I just hoped it wouldn't kill *me*. *Curiosity killed the Jeremy*? I didn't like the sound of that at all.

We paused at the end of the corridor. The growling was coming from beyond the door. Something was on the landing at the top of the stairs.

Despite his bravado, fear flashed into Connor's eyes. Taking a nervy breath, he paused before slowly pushing the door. It opened with a moan. We stepped through the threshold together... and immediately saw what was growling.

At the top of the stairs, a huge window looked out over the grounds. With the curtains open, the moon lit the staircase. And standing on his hind legs, staring out of the window, was Buster, the Bloodhound. His ears were pricked, his muscles tense, every hair on his body standing on end. Growling from deep within his throat, the dog never even glanced our way as we stepped onto the landing, his eyes transfixed on something in the gardens below.

Goosebumps trickled over my skin. I wanted to look out of the window, to see what was causing the fierce rumble from the dog's throat. And yet, at the same time, I didn't.

A nearby grandfather clock ticked. Our shallow breaths rasped. The tense dog growled.

Peering through the window, I tried to see exactly what Buster was staring at but it was hard to tell. Near the castle stood some neatly trimmed rose bushes and next to them, a row of dark trees, including the enormous monkey puzzle tree with its sharp, spiky leaves. In the distance I saw the shower block where we'd camped and, beyond that, the blackness of the woods.

My eyes drifted back to the garden near the castle and as I looked towards the rose bushes again, my eyes caught on something that made my blood run cold.

Amongst the shadows of the monkey puzzle tree, I noticed small clouds of breath being blown into the freezing night air. And as my eyes focused on the darkness, I gradually made out another shape… the shape of a person.

My heart quickened and cold sweat coated my skin. Buster's growling grew louder, his body more rigid. As my eyes adjusted to the gloom, I eventually realised that it was not actually a person out there after all – but a creature, an animal, its face covered with dark hair. The *thing*, with its sharp, snarling teeth and its enormous, spiky antlers protruding from its face, stood there like a human, as tense and angry as Buster. And as I looked into its red eyes, I realised that it was staring right back into mine.

"Do you see that?" Connor whispered. "Is that… is that…?"

Buster's growl deepened.

I held my breath a long moment, scared to exhale.

"It's real," Connor gasped. "Zach was telling the truth."

I gulped as I watched the bizarre creature. Although partly hidden amongst the trees and the midnight darkness, I could still make out its hairy, snarling face and its viciously sharp antlers as it continued to stare in our direction.

Buster – the usually gentle Bloodhound – angrily bared his teeth.

I didn't know what to do. Should we wake up Mr Hopton? Should we bang on the window and try to scare the creature away? Or should we just close our eyes and pretend it wasn't there? I daren't move for fear of angering the thing or causing some sort of terrifying attack on the house.

I was about to ask Connor his thoughts when a strange, unearthly sound came from somewhere downstairs. A weird gurgling that I couldn't quite place. Could a second creature be *inside* the house? Both Connor and I turned to the stairs, gazing into the darkness of the old house. We listened. But nothing stirred. The grandfather clock ticked but no other sounds came.

And then I realised that Buster had stopped growling.

We turned to see his body relax, though clearly still alert. We moved back to the window, looking out towards the trees. But now, the Wendigo, Maureen, was gone.

THURSDAY

CHAPTER THIRTY-ONE: MEESE

"How do you know it was Maureen?" asked Michael. "Maybe it was a bear."

After a breakfast of Coco-Pops and Corn Flakes in the great hall, we'd asked to use the toilet before sneaking outside and heading for the monkey puzzle tree. There was no sun this morning, as usual, just a depressing grey sky and a dampness in the air.

Connor scowled. "There aren't bears in Scotland anymore."

"Besides," I added, "it had these spiky antlers sticking out of its face."

"Well," said Michael, "maybe it was a moose."

"A moose?" Connor hissed. "They don't have meese in Scotland either."

"Meese?" I said. "That's not the right word."

"What is it then?" asked Connor.

"Mice?" suggested Michael.

"No," I said. "Mice means more than one mouse. Is it mooses? Actually, maybe meese is right."

"Stop!" Connor stamped his foot into the squelchy grass. "Can we just keep our eyes on the ball here?"

"What ball?" I said.

"Just focus! The thing we saw *was not* a moose. Its antlers were too vicious and sharp, and were coming out of its cheeks. And it was standing on its back legs – right here." He pointed at the monkey puzzle tree. "Wasn't it, Jeremy?"

I nodded. Weird. He'd called me 'Jeremy', not 'Jellyfish'.

"We have to find out where it went," said Connor, scanning the ground for clues.

"We?" I replied. "I didn't think you wanted anything to do with me? I didn't think you believed in the 'wed-eyed monster'?"

Michael shifted from one foot to the other, avoiding eye-contact.

Connor frowned. "Don't be like that, Jeremy. How were we meant to know that you were telling the truth? You have to admit that it sounded a bit… *crazy*. But now I've seen it with my own eyes. We have to find out where it comes from and where it goes."

"Why?" said Michael, looking alarmed. "If you *did* see it, why can't we just tell the grown-ups?"

"The grown-ups?" Connor scoffed, glaring at Michael as if pink slime had started oozing from his ears. Connor raised a finger in the air. "Firstly, we're not allowed to. Mr Hopton said that if we mention the monster again, he'll send us home."

"And secondly," I added, "the grown-ups aren't being totally honest with us."

Connor frowned. "What do you mean?"

I thought about the I.D. card. The adult with the alternative name and the job at *Frank I.C.G.*, but I didn't want to mention it. Not yet anyway. Despite his sudden change in attitude, I still didn't trust Connor.

"The newspapers," I said. "The ones we found in Zach's room. The newspapers mention Hamish and Zach by name. They *both* knew about the creature when the girls said they'd seen it – but they pretended they didn't. Seems a bit dodgy."

"Zach didn't pretend nothing!" Connor snapped. "Zach was going to tell us about the curse until everyone freaked about the fire on the river."

"Fair enough," I said. "But Hamish knew. And he tried to convince me that I'd seen a stag. And he wears an earring."

"And what about the ginger-haired woman?" said Michael.

"Kat?" I replied. "Yeah, she acted weird when I told her about the dead badger."

I felt relieved that Michael wanted to be involved. He'd been really off with me these past two days. But now we had something in common. We wanted to find Connor's cousin and the truth about the Wendigo.

"So, do you think this creature is killing the animals?" Michael asked.

I shrugged. "Maybe. Badgers, rabbits, frogs. A lot of dead animals around here. And they were dying at the farm before the farmer took them away."

"Yes," said Connor. "But Zach said the animals became ill first. What would that have to do with the Wendigo?"

Michael shrugged. "And what about the missing fur? Buster has bald patches and so did that cat at the farm."

"Who knows," said Connor. "Two things we do know are that Zach is missing and the creature with the antlers is real. If we can find the creature, we'll find Zach. I'm sure of it."

"Okay," I said, feeling weirdly friendly with Connor. "Let's see if we can find any trace of the monster."

We inspected the monkey puzzle tree like a team of experienced detectives. We stared at the branches above our heads before crouching to look at the ground, our eyes scanning the soil.

None of us spoke for a while. I closed my eyes, trying to picture what I'd seen the night before. The clouds of breath puffing from its nose. The tiny red eyes, staring straight at me.

Michael eventually stood up from his crouched position. "Which direction did it go?" he asked.

Connor and I shared a glance.

"Well," I said, "we didn't actually see it go."

"You didn't see it go?" Michael replied.

"We got distracted," I admitted.

"Distracted? Was there something more interesting to look at than a seven-foot bear with antlers in its face?"

Neither of us answered.

Scowling at the ground, Connor crouched.

"Did you see its feet, Jeremy?" he asked.

'Jeremy' again.

I shook my head. I couldn't remember anything about the creature's feet or legs, just that it was standing on two of them. "What do you mean?"

Connor huffed. "What kind of feet did it have? Human feet? Hooves? Paws like a bear? If we can find footprints, we may be able to follow them."

I shook my head. "I don't remember."

Connor sighed. "Okay. Everyone look around. See if you can find anything that shows where it went."

We searched for footprints. It wasn't easy on such a gloomy morning. Lots of leaves had fallen from nearby trees and the soil was bumpy and uneven. I tried moving the leaves around, careful not to disturb any potential evidence. Still, I couldn't see anything resembling a footprint; neither human, hoof, nor paw.

I'd practically run out of patience and was about to give up when I spotted something interesting in the soil: a tiny transparent circle, possibly made of glass or clear plastic.

"I think I've got something," I announced. The others moved closer. I held up a hand to stop them before pointing at the glistening object. Then, as I carefully scooped it up with my finger, the ground juddered... and I thought my life was about to end.

CHAPTER THIRTY-TWO: ABOVE-AVERAGE LEVELS OF GRAVITY

The ground shuddered beneath my feet.

Trees rattled.

I stumbled, almost falling.

Screams came from the castle as the world vibrated like it was about to explode.

As the ground shook angrily one last time, the tiny circle fell from my finger, landing on the grass.

And then… the rumbling stopped.

Apart from leaves falling from the trees and the thrashing of my heartbeat, all was still once more.

"What the hell was that?" said Connor, panting.

"An earthquake," I replied.

"Definitely," Michael added. "I've been in one before."

"No," I said. "You watched a movie about an earthquake. That's not the same."

"It started when you picked that thing up," said Connor.

Gulping deep breaths, we stared down at the small shard of material, roughly the size of a fingernail and perfectly circular.

"It felt moist," I said. "The circle felt moist."

"I think I know what it is," Connor announced. "I think this… is… an inter-dimensional portal."

"I've definitely been in one of those before," said Michael.

"A *portal*?" asked Connor. "A portal to another world?"

"Oh," said Michael. "I thought you said 'portaloo'."

"So… this is a portal to where exactly?" I asked.

"It makes total sense," said Connor, his voice becoming animated. "Last night, when we saw Maureen through the window, we both turned away for a second and when we looked back, the beast was gone. It disappeared into this." He nodded at the little circle, nestled into the grass. "Zach thought that the river was the portal. But I think this tiny disc… could actually be the passage to another world."

Michael and I glanced at each other but didn't speak. Curses, monsters, portals to Hell. I'm not sure this was what Mum imagined when she paid for this trip.

"You had your watch on last night," Connor suddenly said to me. "When did the dog start growling?"

"Thirteen minutes to midnight," I answered, proud to have memorised the time.

"Okay," he said, grinning a reptilian grin. "I have a plan."

*

The zip-line stretched from high up in one enormous pine tree, through the top of the forest, ending at another huge tree in the distance.

"Are you sure you're all okay?" Mr Hopton asked us yet again as we climbed the stairs to the zip-line platform. "Nobody was hurt during the earthquake? No bruises or grazes or anything we need to know about?"

Everyone was fine. Other than the initial scare and shock of the ground rocking, everybody had survived the earthquake without damage.

"I can only apologise," said Hamish, who was with us on the starting platform. "These earthquakes, we've been getting them a lot recently."

"It makes no sense," Nazirah suddenly said to me. "Scotland isn't a country known for having earthquakes. Tokyo, San Francisco, yes. But the Glenkilly region of Scotland?"

I remained silent about touching the transparent coin, the portal to another dimension. Had *it* really caused the earthquake?

Mr Hopton didn't look too comfortable about the whole zip-line situation. "Please make sure they're securely attached," he bleated at Hamish. The instructor just scowled.

Glancing over the edge of the platform, high up in the pine tree, I felt my insides gurgle. The trees below us looked like tiny bits of broccoli and Kat and Mrs Dodd, walking over to the finishing platform, seemed no bigger than insects. An icy wind blew into my face, making me unsteady on my feet.

"I'm not sure I'm brave enough for this," I admitted to Michael.

"Come on, Jeremy. Don't be a wimp."

I frowned. Was that what he really thought?

"This is a Once-in-a-Lifetime Experience," he added.

"Zip-lining? You said you'd done it loads before. You said you zip-lined across the Grand Canyon last year."

"Well… yeah, I did. But I haven't done *this* zip-line."

After waiting an eternity, I eventually arrived at the front of the queue. Hamish fastened me in and assured me over and over again that everything was perfectly safe.

Jumping from the top of a tree, attached to a bit of string, wasn't exactly my idea of fun. I preferred gentler activities, like reading comics and drinking tea.

So it took a lot of mental strength for me to eventually jump from the platform. My guts felt like they'd fallen through my feet as I zoomed through the air. I hated the feeling of the evil wind attacking my face, trying to pull the skin from my cheeks and rip out my hair. If reincarnation was real, I didn't want to come back as a flying squirrel.

When I reached the end of the line, the zip-line bumped into the buffers with a thud. Using a hook on a pole, Kat then pulled me to the finishing platform and unclipped me before sending the harness back to the start.

With my legs still shaking, I watched Michael go next... and I couldn't believe my eyes.

He started well, jumping from the platform and zooming along the wire, just like I had. But then it all went wrong. Instead of speeding up and racing along to the end, the cable sagged.

Michael slowed down.

He slowed some more.

Then some more.

Before eventually stopping, right there in the middle of the zip-line, his feet dangling beneath him, twenty metres above the forest floor.

Kat tutted. "There's always one."

"It makes you wonder," said Mrs Dodd.

"Every time," said Kat, pushing her spectacles up her nose, "there's always one person who doesn't reach the end of the line."

She then rushed down the steps to the bottom of the tree, striding over to the spot where Michael hovered above. She pressed a button on her pole, which extended, before reaching it up to Michael, hooking his harness and dragging him to the end.

When Michael was eventually unclipped, he shook his head. "I knew I wouldn't reach the end of the line… because of my condition."

I raised an eyebrow. "Condition?"

"Yeah, my doctor says I have above-average levels of gravity in my body. The gravity dragged me down and stopped me."

I glanced at Nazirah. She simply shook her head.

CHAPTER THIRTY-THREE: MIDNIGHT IN MY UNDERPANTS

My watch's alarm beeped at 23:25.

Twenty-five past eleven… at night.

"It's time," I announced.

But when I looked up, Michael and Connor were already pulling on their tracky bottoms.

"Hurry, Jeremy," said Connor, now slipping his arms into his coat. "We need to go. Michael, bring your bed sheet. We'll need it for the plan to work."

Quick as a blink, I whipped off my Chewbacca onesie before pulling on a jumper and coat. Michael and Connor waited by the door as I finished putting on my trainers. When I stood up, Michael, who had his rucksack full of essentials, said: "Aren't you forgetting something, Jeremy?"

My brain must have been totally exhausted by this point because when I looked down, I realised that in the rush I'd forgotten to put on any trousers! I was about to take off my shoes again when Connor grabbed my arms and forcefully yanked me through the door.

"We don't have time!" he growled as we tumbled into the dark corridor with a bump. Silence filled the rest of the castle. I wanted to argue and push back into the room. But Connor pulled me and I didn't want to make a commotion and wake anyone up, especially not Mr Hopton.

So that's how I ended up in a Scottish field at a quarter to midnight in my underpants. It wouldn't have been too bad if it wasn't so cold. Sure, my coat kept my chest warm and my feet were dry in my trainers – but my legs were freezing! Standing by the monkey puzzle tree, I would've given anything for a pair of jeans, or trackies, or even a pair of tights!

"What time is it now?" asked Connor, his warm breath clouding in the cold air.

We'd found the tiny transparent circle in the same place we'd left it that morning. I couldn't work out exactly what the thing was – but I actually doubted it was a portal to another dimension. That was just silly talk.

"It's 11:45," I said, holding one corner of Michael's bedsheet.

Connor nodded. "Okay, it's nearly time. Lift the sheet."

Each of us lifted a corner above our heads, high above the little circle nestled into the grass. With only three of us there, one corner sagged, flapping towards the ground.

The plan, according to Connor, was to wait until the Wendigo appeared through this 'magic portal'. Then we'd drop to our knees, trapping the monster in our net... well, Michael's scruffy, stained bedsheet.

"What are we meant to do after that?" I asked.

Connor's eyes narrowed. "Look, if you have a better plan, I'm all ears."

I immediately pictured Connor made entirely of ears but still having a long black fringe. The amusing image was quickly pushed from my mind as a chilling breeze sent a trail of goosebumps racing up my bare legs.

"I could really do with getting some trousers. I think it's going to rain. I can smell it."

"You can't smell rain," scoffed Connor.

"Of course you can," I replied. "It's like a damp smell."

"I can smell snow," said Michael.

"What? Right now?" I asked.

"No. Not now. But when it's coming, I can smell it."

Connor grunted. "Can we concentrate on the task, please?"

Then my watch beeped.

11:47.

We held our breaths.

It was time.

We braced ourselves. Arms tense, eyes wide. Everything around us froze. No sounds from the trees, no whispers from the wind. We stared intensely at the tiny see-through circle.

Watching.

Waiting.

And waiting.

And waiting.

And then we heard the voice.

CHAPTER THIRTY-FOUR: SÉANCE

At thirteen minutes to midnight, the sky was black with thick, dense clouds hiding the moon. No bigger than a penny, the tiny transparent circle lay on the ground near the monkey puzzle tree like a clear, flat fingernail.

We'd braced ourselves for a moment of magic, some sort of sorcery. But there'd been no clouds of smoke. No flashes of bright light. No second earthquake.

Just the voice. A voice I recognised.

"Jeremy?" said Nazirah, from somewhere behind me. "Is that you?"

I turned to see Nazirah's head, wrapped in her purple hijab, poking out of a nearby bush. When she saw my face, she stood up to approach.

Then she stopped.

"Erm, why aren't you wearing any trousers?"

My face flushed. I was standing in a field at night with a bedsheet above my head and nothing on my legs but a pair of Superman underpants.

"We were in a rush," I explained.

"A rush?" Nazirah frowned. "What are you even doing? Is this some sort of séance?"

"What's a séance?" I asked.

"I think it's a French cheese," said Michael.

"No," said Nazirah. "A séance is when you try to contact the dead."

"Well, I suppose we *are* having a séance," I said, "kind of."

"We're not having a blummin' séance!" snapped Connor. He scowled at Nazirah. "Why are *you* here?"

Nazirah shrugged. "I saw you all sneaking out and decided to follow. So… what exactly are you doing with that bedsheet?"

"It's none of your business!" Connor barked. "Go away!"

"We might as well tell her," said Michael. "She's seen too much already."

Nazirah nodded. "Yeah, and if you don't tell me, I could always inform Mr Hopton about your midnight antics."

Connor huffed. "Okay. If you must know, we're waiting to catch the monster that comes through *that* portal." He nodded towards the ground, still holding the bedsheet aloft.

"Portal?" Nazirah moved closer, peering at the damp grass. "What portal? Where?"

"The tiny glass thing," I said. "Connor reckons it's a portal to another world."

She bent down to inspect closer before snorting a laugh. "That's a portal to another world, is it?" She stood up. "I guess you lot have never seen a *contact lense* before."

"Contact lense?" said Connor, his voice filled with disgust.

"That... is a contact lense," Nazirah stated. "My mum wears them."

There was an awkward silence as we stood with the bedsheet still lifted above our heads. Then, realising how silly we must have looked, we lowered the sheet.

"Pass that here," I said, wrapping the sheet around my waist as if it were an ugly skirt from the world's worst fashion show. It warmed my legs, covered my pants and gave me a pinch of dignity.

"Wait a sec," said Nazirah. "What monster are you talking about? The Wendigo?"

"I've told you," said Connor. "This is none of your business. Go. Away."

Nazirah looked hurt, like a scolded puppy.

"Hang on, Connor," I said, leaping to her defence. "I think Nazirah could be a great help here. We all know how smart she is. She even knows the seven-times table."

Michael and Connor gasped.

"If you want to find out what's happened to Zach," I went on, "I think we need to tell Nazirah everything."

"Zach?" said Nazirah. "What *has* happened to him?"

"Jeremy's right," said Michael. "We should tell her."

I nodded at Michael. He nodded back. Maybe we *were* still best friends after all.

Following a great sigh, Connor finally agreed to tell Nazirah the whole story. About the legend of the Glenkilly Curse. About the sightings of Maureen; through the window and at the abandoned farm. We told her about the bubbling river and the farmer's sickly animals. I even dared to mention the newspaper reports again.

"And Zach's been missing for two whole days," said Connor, concluding the recap of events. "He could be hurt or imprisoned or…" His voice broke and he didn't finish the sentence.

"So the monster was here?" asked Nazirah.

I nodded. "Yeah."

"So, why would it wear a contact lense?"

Nobody answered.

As a cruel wind whipped into our faces, I thought it was time to show Michael and Connor what else I'd found. I pulled the wallet from my coat pocket, showing it to the others.

Connor frowned, confused by the I.D. card. "What the –?"

"Something strange is going on at *Frank I.C.G.*," I said.

"I don't think it's a conservation company," added Nazirah.

"And that's the 'Executive Site Manager'," I said, pointing at the I.D. card in Connor's hand.

"So what does this mean?" asked Michael.

I shrugged. Nazirah shook her head, baffled.

"I'm not sure," said Connor, sweeping the black fringe from his face. "But I think we need to go over there and take a look. Maybe Zach stuck his nose into something he wasn't meant to. Maybe he got too close to the truth."

"Right," I said. "Do you think I've got time to nip inside and fetch some trousers? It's pretty cold and it's going to rain."

"It's not going to rain," Connor snorted. "We need to get to *Frank I.C.G.*"

"Okay. But…" I hesitated. "Shouldn't we check the farm first? That's where we last saw him. He might still be there, injured or something."

"I agree with Jeremy," said Nazirah. "Even though I'm suspicious of *Frank I.C.G.*, we should check the farm first."

Connor shook his head. "Zach won't be injured. He's a grown man with armpit hair and everything. We need to get onto this conservation site to see what they're up to." Connor's eyes became thoughtful. "Tell you what, why don't you and Nazirah go to the farm. Me and Michael can check out this Frank place."

"No!" I blurted, far too quickly.

Everyone eyed me curiously. I knew that checking the farm first was the sensible move; Zach could still be there, stuck down a hole or snagged in a bear trap. We *had* to look there first before going off to explore the conservation site. But I couldn't bear the thought of Connor taking Michael off on his own, filling his head with cruel whispers about me, Elbow-Bumping my best friend out of my life.

"You're absolutely right," I said. "Zach won't be at the farm. Let's get into *Frank I.C.G.*, pronto."

Nazirah watched me with suspicion as we stepped away from the monkey puzzle tree, towards the blackness of the woods… just as the first raindrops began to fall. I knew I could smell it.

CHAPTER THIRTY-FIVE: CLIVE THE CYGNET

Frank I.C.G.'s fence stood at the north edge of the complex, meaning we had to traipse through the woods to get there.

A dense ceiling of leaves draped the ground in shadows that stretched and twisted as Connor's torchlight pierced the dark while strange animals yipped and yelped, putting us all on edge. I knew they were just nocturnal rodents but a ripple of doubt gnawed at me. Could it be Maureen? Was the vicious Wendigo about to charge through the undergrowth and flip us into the air with its deadly antlers?

We trudged on. The damp ground seeped into my trainers and flecks of mud splashed at my ankles (and onto Michael's bedsheet). Light sprinkles of raindrops snuck through the leaves, a whiff of rotten eggs drifted through the air and in the distance I could hear the gentle slosh of the river.

Connor suddenly glanced my way, his eyes wide with fear.

"Jeremy! Behind you!"

My heart almost shot through my chest. I ducked, wincing, jumping off the path into a wet bush. Frozen, frightened, my hands clutched my head in a defensive brace. I looked up, expecting to have some wild, snarling beast attack me… instead, I heard Connor cackling.

"Ha! Did you see that? He's such a wuss!"

Glowering, I climbed to my feet, wiping the damp from my coat. The bedsheet around my legs was now wet through. My face glowed with – what? Rage? Embarrassment? Even in a time as tense as this, Connor somehow found the energy to make a fool of me.

Today, I'd naively thought he'd changed, that we had some kind of bond since we'd seen the Wendigo together. I guess a leopard can't change its spots.

And now, as I glanced along the path, I saw the leopard wandering off, patting my best friend on the back. I wouldn't let Connor get away with this. Nazirah smiled at me sadly before we continued through the woods.

After Connor's prank, none of us spoke for a while; alert, focused, afraid. As we trampled through the nettles and bracken, I checked my watch. 00:21. Twenty-one minutes past midnight. I could probably count on one hand the number of times I'd been up this late (and on none of those occasions had I been in the middle of a Scottish forest with no adults).

A gentle hand suddenly took hold of my elbow. Nazirah held me back, leaving the others to march ahead.

"What was that all about?" she whispered. "Changing your mind about the farm. You know that was the best option. Why the sudden change?"

I hesitated before answering. "I just think we should stick together."

Nazirah frowned, unconvinced. "Yeah but why not stick together *and* visit the farm first? You didn't put up much of an argument."

I shrugged. "Michael and Connor wanted to come here. I couldn't just let them go off together."

"Oh, I see," said Nazirah. "You're jealous."

I stopped walking. "*What?*"

"You're jealous of Michael and Connor."

I pretended to laugh. "That's ridiculous. Why would I be jealous of those two?"

"You don't want them to be friends."

"Well, no. Of course I don't. Michael is *my* friend, not Connor's. Connor's an idiot. Everyone knows *that*. You saw what he just did to me."

Nazirah narrowed her eyes but didn't answer. We carried on walking. The other two were far ahead now.

"But surely Michael can be friends with whoever he likes," Nazirah said eventually.

I couldn't work out if this was a statement or a question. I answered anyway. "Yes. But not Connor. Connor hates me. I can't let Michael be friends with him."

"But you can't stop him either. You don't own Michael. You can't control your friends. That's not how it works." She paused for a moment, allowing the thought to sink in.

An owl hooted somewhere in the distance and the volume of the river increased from a gentle whisper to a loud rush. It was close by. The ground underfoot had softened to a wet mulch as rain trickled through from the leaves above.

Then Nazirah said something totally random.

"I rescued a cygnet once."

I frowned. "You rescued a cigarette?"

"No. A cygnet. A baby swan. All on its own near Foster Pond. No mum, no brothers or sisters. And it was limping."

"What did you do?" I asked, even though I had no idea why she was telling me this.

"I took him home and named him Clive. I kept him warm and safe. Clive probably would've died on his own. A fox or a big fish might've eaten him. My dad's a vet, so he knew what to do."

"So you've got a pet swan called Clive?"

Nazirah laughed. "No. You see, that's the thing. Clive had to be set free. He had to learn about the world for himself, find his own friends, work out who he needed to avoid. If Clive had stayed with us, he wouldn't have learned anything about the real world, not properly anyway."

I scratched my neck. "I'm not being funny, Nazirah, but we're in the middle of these woods, where there's a monster with antlers coming out of its face. I can't really see what a baby swan has got to do with anything."

"Jeremy, I didn't want to let that swan leave. I was worried it would get into all sorts of trouble and I knew that the safest place for it would be with me. Clive was my best friend in the world but I knew that he had to make his own way in life."

The rain splashed a little harder through the trees, dampening our clothes and skin. Then the penny dropped, like an elephant jumping into a swimming pool.

"Okay, I get it. You're saying I should just give up. You're saying I should lose my best friend?"

Nazirah shook her head. "I'm not saying that you give up on your best friend. Just try not to smother him. Let him be friends with other people. You and Michael are *best friends*, there's no denying that. When you're at school, you stick together like cyanoacrylate."

"Like *what?*"

"Super Glue."

"Oh."

"You're the bestest of best mates. But sometimes it's healthy to have other friends too."

"What – even Connor?"

Nazirah nodded. "Maybe you should actually *talk* to Connor. I think his heart is in the right place, even if his ideas are sometimes a bit... reckless."

"He just made me jump into a soaking bush for no good reason."

Nazirah half-shrugged. "Talk to him. Try and get to the bottom of your problems."

I sighed and was about to answer when I noticed that the other two were standing statue still at a clearing in the woods. We moved towards them and, as the trees thinned out, I saw that we'd arrived at a giant mesh fence, where the grounds of Glenkilly Castle ended. The land on the other side of that fence belonged to the conservation company, *Frank I.C.G.*.

We covered our noses.

Michael spoke. "It smells like mouldy egg sandwiches! Somebody should be arrested for Grievous Bodily Farts!"

"D'ya think there's a way in?" asked Connor.

We stepped out from the shadows, surveying the huge fence. It must have been ten metres tall, with barbed-wire at the top. There were no signs of any gates. All we could see through the fence were dark trees. Whatever they had over there – near the strange tower and the filthy pond – was hidden for the time-being by the thick forest.

We stood in silence, wondering what to do.

And then something came crashing through the trees.

CHAPTER THIRTY-SIX: GAS LEAK

None of us dared breathe.

Hidden behind the trunk of a thick oak tree, we peered at the mesh fence across the clearing. Something trampled through the undergrowth. Twigs snapped, leaves rustled, wet breath panted. A lump hardened in my throat as I braced myself to see some unearthly creature charge through the woods.

And then it appeared.

Sharp, shiny eyes, like marbles reflected the moonlight. Hot, damp breath clouded the air. And then the furry brown creature came into full view.

Only it wasn't the Wendigo.

This animal stood just a metre tall – on all fours.

A dog. A German Shepherd, to be precise. The sort the police have. It sniffed the ground near the fence, where we'd just been standing. Could it smell us? Watching the thick-coated creature nosing the grass, I noticed bald patches across the dog's brown and black fur.

Moments later, a second dog rushed through the bracken before sniffing the same spot… then came a man. The man strolled by the dogs, not paying them any attention. He moved slowly. Tall and heavy-looking, he had the word '*SECURITY*' stitched across his black jacket. A walkie-talkie crackled a couple of times as he passed.

Attached to the left side of the security guard's belt was a long, thick metallic pole with a handle attached to it. It was some sort of baton like the ones police officers might use… and extremely dangerous in the wrong hands.

But the most noticeable, most terrifying feature of the guard's outfit was on his head. None of us could see the man's face, making him impossible to identify, because over his head he wore a gas mask; an old-fashioned sort like those from World War Two.

We watched this frightening figure in horror. He clicked his fingers twice, a command the dogs understood. They raced off to the next crowd of trees and instantly vanished, swallowed up by the darkness.

Nazirah gasped. "What. The. Actual. Heck."

"Why is he wearing that mask?" I asked.

"Gas leak or something," said Nazirah. "You can smell it."

I thought of the bubbling river and the fire that Michael had lit. I'd expected Connor to repeat his nonsense about smelling the devil – but he didn't say a thing. He looked worried.

"Do you think it's safe to be here?" asked Nazirah. "*Frank I.C.G.* claim to be a conservation company. They're meant to protect wildlife. But you've seen the site next door."

"The pond looked disgusting," I agreed, "filled with rubbish. And that strange mist."

"So it's *not* a conservation site," said Nazirah. "We can be certain of that."

"Even if it was, why would they need a security team with dogs and weapons?"

"Exactly."

I reached into my pocket and pulled out the wallet. Opening it up, I stared at the I.D. card inside.

Executive Site Manager. Frank I.C.G.

And there was the face we knew so well. But why? Why did this person, who we trusted, have an important job with *Frank I.C.G.*? We felt sure that *Frank I.C.G.* wasn't actually a conservation company. So what was it? And what on Earth was this person playing at?

The rain lightly pitter-pattered the leaves above us. Nazirah stared hard at the ground for a long moment before speaking.

"I think," she said, "anyone who works for *Frank I.C.G.* must know all about the strange happenings at Glenkilly Castle; the monster, the abandoned farm, the bubbling river. Maybe they're investigating what's going on, like we are."

"Okay," I said. "But if *Frank I.C.G.* are the good guys, then where's Zach?"

"Exactly," said Connor. "Jellyfish is right… for once."

Back to 'Jellyfish'.

Nazirah shrugged. "Zach may still be at the farm for all we know, which is why we should've checked there first."

A knot tightened in my stomach. Something wasn't right. I wished we'd never got involved in this business. Mythical monsters, suspicious companies, bubbling rivers. All I'd wanted from this trip was to become a little braver – by making it halfway up the climbing wall or trying Irn-Bru – not by actually facing death.

"Something fishy is going on at *Frank I.C.G.*," said Connor. "They have my cousin. I know it. We need to get in there."

Moving away from the oak tree, we stepped back into the clearing. The moon provided a slither of light. Connor turned on his torch and we reassessed the massive fence.

"How are we meant to get through?" I asked.

"It's too high to climb," said Nazirah.

"If we had a spade, we could dig under," said Connor.

"But we don't," I replied.

"I have some bolt cutters," said Michael.

We ignored him. Michael always claimed to have the oddest things; a ghost-detecting machine, a Spanish-speaking dolphin, a psychic cactus that can predict football results.

We stood for a moment longer, scratching our heads and twiddling our thumbs, before we heard an odd snipping sound. We turned to see Michael clipping a big hole in the wire mesh fence with a pair of industrial bolt cutters.

"Are you allowed to do that?" asked Nazirah. "Isn't that… criminal damage?"

"Never mind that," said Connor. "My cousin's life is on the line!"

"Where did you get those snippers from?" I asked.

"Bolt cutters?" Michael answered. "My bag. I just told you I had them but nobody listened."

"What else do you have in there?" asked Connor.

Michael peered into his rucksack. "Swiss Army Knife, twenty-seven pence, pyjama bottoms, cigarette lighter, Pokémon cards, sunflower seeds, thimbles, golden syrup, bouncy balls, string and a voucher for a Big Mac."

"You have pyjama bottoms?" I asked.

He nodded, smiling proudly. "Prepared for all situations."

My mouth slowly opened. "Then why do I have a bedsheet wrapped around my waist?"

Michael looked embarrassed – like he was struggling to add two and two in front of a large crowd – before finally passing me the bottoms.

"Be careful with them," he said. "They're my third best pair."

Nazirah looked away while I replaced my makeshift skirt with the bottoms.

Once Michael had snipped a hole big enough for an average ten-year-old, we stood staring through the gap. Tense, terrified. What would we find on the other side? The monster? An evil scientist conjuring it up? A dark truth about Connor's cousin? Or something else entirely?

Somewhere behind us, the river still gushed in the distance. But ahead, beyond the fence and the dark trees, I heard something else. A low hum. Something mechanical, perhaps? We stood in silence a moment longer, staring into the woods beyond the fence… and then I excitedly grabbed Connor by the arm.

"Connor, I just saw Zach. He was right there," I lied, pointing at the black trees on the other side of the fence.

"I didn't see anything," said Michael.

"Nor did I," Connor agreed.

"He was moving fast. Running. Like he was in a rush. Maybe he's in trouble. Or being chased."

I heard Connor's breathing tighten, almost panting. As he climbed through the hole in the fence, I had to stifle a laugh. Of course, I *hadn't* seen Zach at all. But this would teach him. For making me jump into a wet bush for no good reason. For calling me 'Jellyfish' all the time. For trying to steal my best friend.

"Where was he?" Connor asked, his voice high with panic, his anxious eyes scouring the dark, empty scene in search of his cousin.

"Right there," I lied, pointing again. "He went that way. Moving fast."

As Connor stepped towards the dark woods, Michael also pulled himself through the gap.

"What are *you* doing?" I asked.

Michael scowled. "Going to help Connor. Aren't you coming?"

I tried not to grin. This was so funny. "Maybe you should just wait here." Everyone would laugh so hard when they realised it was all a prank – and, for once, Connor had made himself look silly, all frightened and panicked, instead of me.

"Nah," said Michael. "We should help. Come on." He marched after Connor. I didn't like seeing them side-by-side, but this was going to be hilarious...

I held Nazirah back, smiling.

"See. I'm letting them go off together. I'm not being jealous at all."

Nazirah frowned. "I hope this is not some sort of stupid trick, Jeremy."

I didn't answer. Just grinned. How could I reveal that this was just a joke? Shout *'Boo!'*? Or just start laughing? I didn't do pranks very often so I wasn't sure.

Nazirah stayed quiet for a moment, watching Connor and Michael approach the darkness. Then she turned to me. "Jeremy. About that contact lense you found…"

She didn't get chance to finish her sentence, however, because a sharp scream suddenly shattered the night air. The noise cut through the forest before being instantly muffled. My eyes flashed to the spot where Michael and Connor had just been standing.

They weren't there.

Something was carrying them both. A huge, antlered figure, running like a human. One child in each arm. I saw it for less than a second before it was gone. Vanished into the black shadows of the forest.

CHAPTER THIRTY-SEVEN: IRONING SOCKS

His eyes barely open, Mr Hopton opened his bedroom door wearing an ugly pair of brown Y-fronts, a moth-eaten vest and a confused expression. Nazirah wasn't sure where to look.

After racing back to the castle and sneaking in through a door that we'd left open, we'd knocked on our teacher's door at the end of the boys' corridor.

"Why are you two awake?" he asked, glancing down the dark, silent hallway. "Don't you know the time?"

"Yes," I said, glancing at my watch. "It's twenty-three minutes to one."

"It's Connor and Michael," said Nazirah. "They've been taken."

Mr Hopton opened his mouth and then closed it again.

"It was the Wendigo," I blurted out. "We saw it!"

Confused, Mr Hopton's forehead crinkled like a paper bag. "What?"

"The monster!" I yelled.

Mr Hopton snapped a finger to his lips. "Shhh!" Again, his eyes flashed along the corridor. No one stirred. Wrapping a dressing gown around himself, our teacher ushered us into his room. Although immaculately tidy, the room smelled of sweaty socks, stale breath and stress.

"You can't make that kind of noise in the middle of the night, Jeremy. And what have I told you about mentioning the monster. Do I need to send you home?"

"Mr Hopton, it's true," said Nazirah. "I saw it with my own eyes."

Mr Hopton glared at Nazirah – like rabbit ears had just popped out the top of her head.

"Nazirah Hameed, you're normally the most sensible girl in our class. You don't usually hang around with these…" He gestured a hand in my direction. "… these… *characters*."

"Mr Hopton, it's true," she repeated.

Our teacher vigorously rubbed his eyes, as if to wake himself from a dream. He shook his head, perching himself on the edge of his bed before speaking. "Right. Start from the beginning. What on earth are you talking about?"

Nazirah looked at me. I nodded. It would be better coming from her.

"Okay," she said. "So, about an hour ago, we went off into the woods."

Mr Hopton sprang to his feet. "*What? Why?*"

Nazirah showed her palms in a calming motion. "Connor was worried about his cousin, who's now been missing for more than twenty-four hours. Plus, we've found some strange clues regarding the conservation company next door, *Frank I.C.G.* So, we decided to… investigate."

"Why didn't you mention any of this to me?" Mr Hopton snapped. "I could have helped."

"Because it all relates to the Wendigo," I said. "Maureen."

Mr Hopton arched a flaky eyebrow. "Maureen? My name's John, not Maureen."

John? Weird. I didn't think teachers were allowed first names.

Nazirah shook her head. "The Wendigo is an antlered creature from North American mythology. It eats people. Over here they call it Maureen."

I chipped in. "You told me that I wasn't allowed to mention the creature again. So we couldn't tell you."

"So what?" said Mr Hopton. "You went looking for this creature on your own? In the middle of the night? That was a ridiculous idea!"

"No," said Nazirah. "We were looking for Connor's cousin. We had our suspicions that *Frank I.C.G.* is hiding something, so we went there. When Michael and Connor entered the premises, they were immediately snatched by… *something*."

"It was the Wendigo!" I said.

Mr Hopton frowned. It was a dark and stormy frown, full of wrinkles and flaky skin. He switched his gaze to Nazirah. "Was it really this… *Wendy-Cup*?"

"Wendigo!" I said.

Nazirah gulped and then slowly nodded. "I think so. It was big, upright like a human and it *did* seem to have antlers. It was hard to tell. It moved fast. And it snatched Michael and Connor."

"It *was* the Wendigo. I've been seeing it all week."

Mr Hopton paced the room, taking deep breaths. He marched over to his wardrobe, pulled out an ironing board and unfolded it. Without speaking, he took out an iron, filled it with water and plugged it in. Then he went to one of his drawers.

"What are you doing?" asked Nazirah.

"I'm going to iron my socks," he replied. "In times of stress, ironing helps me relax… to think clearly."

"We don't have time!" I snapped. "Michael has been taken. He could be…"

I'd tried to hold it together but everything suddenly overwhelmed me. Tears gushed from my eyes. My throat felt hard as a rock. This was all my fault. I'd lied to Michael and Connor, pretending I'd seen Zach. Now they could be prisoners, injured… dead. I gave out a short wail.

Nazirah placed a hand on my shoulder. "We have to call the police."

"Yes," said Mr Hopton, smoothing out a sock on the ironing board. "You're right." He moved back to the wardrobe and pulled out a pair of jeans. "I'll go and wake Hamish."

"No!" Nazirah and I spoke at the same time.

Mr Hopton frowned. "But we need to call the police?"

"Yes," said Nazirah, "but we're not sure who we can trust here. The staff members appear to have other interests. Interests in *Frank I.C.G.*"

"But –" Mr Hopton tried to argue but I cut him off.

"Let's just call the police without waking anyone."

Mr Hopton's frown deepened. He clearly couldn't believe what had happened. One minute, he was in a peaceful sleep. Now this. Two missing children.

"Okay," he said eventually. "But I'm waking Mrs Dodd."

*

"It makes you wonder," said Mrs Dodd, shaking her head.

The offices near the main entrance were all locked, so we had no access to the phones there. Luckily, an old-fashioned payphone was attached to the wall near the door. Even more luckily, calls to 999 were free.

I listened to Mr Hopton explain the situation down the phone.

"Two children missing…

Snatched in the night…

Glenkilly Castle."

When he replaced the handset, he didn't look pleased.

"They didn't sound very keen on coming," he said to Mrs Dodd. "Kept saying *'again?'* and even said they wouldn't rush to get here."

My mind flashed back to the news article I'd read in Zach's room.

*We are a small force and an hour's round-trip
to Glenkilly Castle is a waste of precious time.*

The police weren't going to rush. How long would they take? An hour? Two? What had I done? I'd been the one constantly going on about this stupid creature in the woods. I'd become obsessed to the point that I'd dragged Michael and Connor into it. And I'd become jealous. I'd pushed Michael away, become overbearing. And if it wasn't for me, he wouldn't have followed Connor through that fence. My body began to shake. I couldn't just sit here and wait for the police to waddle up in a couple of hours when it might be too late. I clenched my fists. I had to act now.

"Should we ring the parents?" Mr Hopton was asking Mrs Dodd.

"I think we have to," she replied.

While they were in serious discussions about what to do next, I grabbed Nazirah by the arm.

Without making a sound, we left.

CHAPTER THIRTY-EIGHT: GIANT FART MONSTER

My mouth was thick with spittle, my throat hurt and my lungs burned. As we sprinted back to the fence beyond the woods, I barely thought of the dangers that may have lurked in the darkness. My mind focused on one thing only: saving Michael.

Mr Hopton would probably be wondering where we'd vanished to. Panicking even more. His face red, his hair turning greyer by the second. I didn't care. We couldn't just wait for the police. We had to do *something*.

My eyes watered against the cold wind as we raced through the woods. Still in my coat and Michael's pyjama bottoms, I darted for the hole that Michael had cut in the fence.

Nazirah placed a hand on my arm. "Jeremy, we have to be careful."

I nodded before climbing through. The pyjama bottoms snagged slightly on the fence. We crept through the trees, occasionally pausing to listen for security guards or dogs or

Maureen. The stink of stale gas grew stronger, as if we were approaching the lair of a giant fart monster.

Strangely, the further we trampled through the undergrowth, the brighter the woods became. Lights shone in a clearing ahead. The low rumble of power generators hummed and the occasional clatter of metal banged and bashed. People were working, even at this late hour. 00:58 according to my watch, almost one o'clock in the morning. Realising the time, I yawned – but shook the tiredness away; I had to stay sharp… for Michael.

Just ahead, we saw an opening in the trees; a large space bathed in spotlights. I watched Nazirah's face as she took in the scene, her mouth slowly dropping open. It was the site I'd seen from the Games Room; the Lookout Tower, the cylinder buildings, the filthy pond. And, now stronger than ever, the potent stench of rotten eggs.

Nazirah's light brown skin had drained of so much colour, she looked grey.

"Oh dear," she said, shaking her head. "I know what this place is. Of course. It was so obvious from the start."

I nodded. "Of course!" I had no idea what she was talking about.

"That name. *Frank I.C.G.* It's hardly a good disguise, is it?"

I fake-laughed. "I know." I wished she'd just get on with her explanation.

"All you have to do is take the N and swap it with the C. And it all becomes clear."

"So obvious," I agreed, nodding along. "So obviously clear... what's so clear?"

"*Frank I.C.G.* Swap the N for the C and the word becomes *Frack I.N.G.* Fracking!"

I grinned. "Ohhh... What's that?"

"This *isn't* a conservation company. It's a fracking site."

"Of course! What's that?"

"Hydraulic Fracturing. Fracking. This is a fracking site."

I frowned. "Franking site? Isn't he the monster with the bolts in his neck?"

"Not franking. Frack-ing! Energy companies think fracking is a way of getting cheap gas from deep within the Earth. They drill deep, deep holes and then flush huge amounts of water and chemicals down those holes. The pressure from this cracks the rock underground, which then releases the gas."

I shrugged. "So what's the problem?"

"You've seen it for yourself," said Nazirah. "The river is bubbling. We're not allowed to drink the tap water. The water

235

here is contaminated. The air too. That's why the guard wore a gas mask."

I suddenly felt dizzy.

"And think about the animals," Nazirah went on. "They're all losing their fur. They're sick, just like those dead rabbits. No wonder the farmer moved his livestock elsewhere."

"So it had nothing to do with the phone lines?"

"No. The land was being fracked all along. And they're clearly not meant to be doing it here. It's not being regulated. That's why they've been having earthquakes. That's why they're going under a fake name."

My gut churned. A huge energy company was running an illegal drilling operation that nobody knew about. This was serious. This was seriously serious. I felt more scared than the time I watched *'Gremlins 2'*. But what did this have to do with the Wendigo?

"So," I whispered, "the fire at the river and the bubbles. They were caused by this fracking business?"

Nazirah nodded. "Most probably. If gas has been released from the ground, it would explain why the river bubbled and why you could set it alight."

"So it had nothing to do with the Glenkilly Curse? Or demons from an underworld?"

Nazirah wrinkled her nose. "I highly doubt it."

"And the rabbits weren't killed by Maureen? They were just sick?"

"Probably."

"So how does the monster fit into all of this? Why was it lurking on this site? And why has it taken Michael and Connor?"

Nazirah shrugged. "No idea."

Inspecting the buildings near the dirty pond, my eyes fixed on a small porta-cabin. I tapped Nazirah's arm before nodding in the cabin's direction. Cautiously, we approached the edge of the clearing through the thistles and the mulch of fallen leaves. We tiptoed to the porta-cabin like a pair of church mice, ducking into the darkest shadows as the rain continued to launch itself at the ground. The rotten-egg stench became almost unbearable and I wished we had gas masks for ourselves now.

Pressing our backs to the wall, the vast open space stood in front of us with the filthy pond in the centre and the weird Lookout Tower across the way. Michael had first compared the scaffolded structure to the Eiffel Tower in Paris. Now, in the brooding darkness, it looked far more threatening and sinister – like that one in Blackpool.

"That must be the drilling rig," whispered Nazirah, nodding towards the tower.

"So it's not a Lookout Tower?"

Nazirah shook her head. "It's a drilling rig. They drill deep holes from there and then send the water down. That 'fractures' the Earth, which is where they get the name 'fracking' from. I should've known as soon as I saw the tower. I'm such an idiot."

I placed my hand on her shoulder. "You're not an idiot, Nazirah. You're a genius. You know twelve times three. And I bet you know the capital of Paris."

"Jeremy, Paris isn't a countr–"

"And I bet you can spell spaghetti."

Nazirah smiled. "Yes, I can spell spaghetti. Thanks, Jeremy."

We flinched when a loud thud boomed by the side of the cabin – a door opening.

Someone was coming!

After diving behind a thick crowd of ferns to hide, we could hear the puffing and panting of wet breath.

The person sounded angry and flustered.

However, when the person charged around the corner, we immediately saw that it wasn't actually a *person* at all.

CHAPTER THIRTY-NINE: BLACK REEBOK TRAINERS

It's not every day that you come face-to-face with a hideous, hairy, snarling creature with vicious, spiky antlers growing from its cheeks... or in the case of our trip to Glenkilly, it actually *is* every day.

Maureen stood right before us as we hid behind the ferns. This was the closest we'd been to the Wendigo, now clear to see in the drilling area's floodlights. Its body – although human in the way it moved – was covered in jet black hair. Its torso, though, was hairless, showing a dark grey chest and belly, just like a gorilla. I could even see its nipples.

I trembled as Maureen surveyed the area with its bright red eyes. Its hot breath clouded the cold air. My guts clenched.

All we had to do right now was remain absolutely still and silent... but then I farted.

I couldn't help it!

And it wasn't a '*silent-but-deadly*' either; more like an out-of-tune blast on a saxophone.

Maureen's head flashed towards us, its red eyes pausing on the ferns but giving no indication as to whether it could see us or not. My heart pounded. Maureen held its gaze on us for a moment before eventually looking away.

Then, taking great strides, the monster squelched off through the mud and the beating rain. And as it disappeared around the cabin corner, I noticed something weird.

Another door slammed. The beast had gone inside.

Nazirah and I exhaled for the first time in what had felt like five minutes – but was probably ten seconds.

"Nice time to let rip," said Nazirah.

We both giggled before pausing to process what we'd just seen... in particular, one small detail.

"Did you see its feet?" I asked.

"The trainers?" said Nazirah. "A wild, terrifying monster that's supposedly been haunting these woods for hundreds of years was wearing trainers. Black Reebok trainers. Do you know what this means, Jeremy?"

I nodded. "Maureen must be ancient. Reebok hasn't been in fashion since the nineties."

Nazirah sighed. "It's a woodland beast. Why is it even wearing trainers?"

"And if it lives in the woods," I added, "when did it learn to open doors? What's it doing inside this cabin?"

A cold moment of silence passed before a porta-cabin window slid open to our left. A light flickered on inside. Cautiously, we stepped up to the window, peering in to see a plain, white-walled, barely-furnished room – like a prison cell, or a teachers' staff room. A single light bulb hung from the ceiling, giving off a pale yellow glow – no lampshade (Granny wouldn't have approved).

In one corner, the security guard we'd seen earlier sat hunched over a desk that was littered with papers and maps. He faced away from us, so we could see the word *SECURITY* on the back of his coat. With his gas mask now removed, I could see grey flecks in his hair and would guess his age at around fifty. He was reading documents and filling in forms. No sign of the dogs, thank goodness.

Next to the desk stood a tall filing cabinet. There were two doors, one at each end of the room, and stuck to the wall, almost like wallpaper, were maps and notices with the following headings:

PHASE ONE
PHASE TWO
PHASE THREE
PHASE FOUR

An icy gasp then caught in my chest as I glanced across the room.

Connor –like some sort of prisoner – was tied to a rusty radiator with a piece of rope. He looked petrified; tears filled his eyes. Where was Michael? Where was Zach? Guilt stabbed in my gut. This was all my fault. Seeing Connor there, tied up, frightened, I realised how wrong I'd been. I'd suspected him and Zach of being involved with the monster. But how could they be? If Zach was involved, why would the beast have snatched Connor? Why would he be tied up?

I waved, trying to get his attention – but he didn't notice. I wanted to knock on the window but the guard would have heard. We had to get him out of there as quickly as possible and find out what they'd done with Michael. But how? Could we sneak in and free them without the guard noticing? Almost impossible. Perhaps we could cause a distraction, get the guard out of the room and then free Connor. But what about Maureen? I wasn't sure where the creature had gone. Was the guard somehow related to the Wendigo? Was *he* a sort of Dr Jekyll?

Rain hammered noisily against the ground. We had to get Connor out. I was about to ask Nazirah her thoughts when the guard suddenly stood up, large and looming over Connor. And then he began to interrogate our classmate, while all we could do was watch through the glass.

CHAPTER FORTY: PIGGIN' LIES

"How much do you know?" the guard growled at Connor, his voice rougher than sandpaper and rasping with anger. Without the gas mask on, we saw that he was unshaven with a mop of messy black-but-greying hair on his head. His teeth were crooked and nicotine-stained.

Nazirah and I were watching through the cabin window as the scene unfolded.

Connor answered with a whimper. "Nothing. I don't know nothing."

"Liar! You're a piggin' liar! You two little swamp-rats wouldn't be snoopin' on our property if you didn't know somethin'. The Boss didn't bring you in here for no piggin' reason!"

I flashed Nazirah a glance. The Boss? But hadn't the *beast* grabbed Michael and Connor? I could've sworn that's what I'd seen; the antlered creature carrying them off through the woods.

"I don't know nothing," said Connor, his voice laced with fear. "I'm just looking for my cousin. Zach McCafferty. Do you know him?"

The guard growled. "You're a piggin' liar! The Boss will want to know precisely how much you know, so you'd best start telling the piggin' truth."

The Boss?

I thought of the I.D. card.

Executive Site Manager.

"Any lies to The Boss," the guard went on, "and you'll be in trouble deeper than the hole we're going to dig through the middle of Glenkilly Castle."

Nazirah and I looked at each other with wide eyes. A hole through Glenkilly Castle? Why? They already had a hole here, didn't they?

"What do you know?" the guard growled again. "If you don't start tellin' the truth, I'm going to start cuttin' off toes."

Outside, we ducked beneath the window, exchanging a frightened glance.

"The guy's insane," Nazirah whispered in a fragile whisper. "We need to help Connor."

"How though?" I asked.

"I have a plan. There are two doors, right? I'll go to one and distract him."

"No! Too dangerous!"

She ignored me. "You sneak in the other door and untie Connor. Wait for my signal."

"What signal?" I asked.

"I'll make a noise like the Black-browed Albatross of Southern Chile."

"*What?* How am I supposed to know what that sounds like?"

Pulling me away from the open window, Nazirah then made a horrible noise that sounded like a seagull crossed with a T-Rex, being strangled to death.

"*Shhhhh!*" I hissed, staring at her in disbelief. "Be quiet or the guard will hear. Anyway, I'm not doing that. It's too weird."

"Fine, I'll do the mating call of the Madagascan Fossa?"

"I don't know that either!"

Nazirah sighed, visibly disappointed by my lack of animal knowledge. "Okay, Jeremy. Just listen for the bangs. When you hear three loud bangs, make your way inside."

With that, she cautiously crept off to my left, leaving me to sneak to the other side. Approaching the door silently, I wrapped my hand carefully around the handle. The worst possible thing now would be for the guard to come charging out. Well, the *worst* possible thing would be for Maureen to appear and bite off my leg, or for aliens to suddenly blow up the Earth, or for Mr Hopton to come around the corner with a test on fractions. But the guard coming through the door would be pretty bad.

Listening in silence, barely breathing, I waited for the right moment. Rain beat against the ground and a soft wind whirled through the trees. The guard's gravelly voice continued to growl on the other side of the door.

Until…

BANG! BANG! BANG!

That was my cue.

I counted to three then gently pushed the door open. As I peered into the room, I saw the guard vanishing through the opposite door.

"Hello?" he called into the darkness, investigating the banging. "Is somebody there?"

And then he was gone, disappearing into the midnight rain, the door slamming shut behind him.

I rushed into the room.

Connor's eyes widened when he saw me, half with joy, half with fear, like he'd just watched an episode of the Teletubbies for the first time.

Tugging and twisting, I tried to untie the rope around his wrists. It gradually came loose before dropping to the floor. Connor stood up, rubbing his wrists.

"Thanks," he said, the relief of freedom bringing a rush of colour to his cheeks.

I didn't answer. Like a moth to a light, my eyes had been instantly attracted to the papers on the wall.

PHASE ONE
PHASE TWO
PHASE THREE
PHASE FOUR

I ripped the sheets down to read. It was mostly technical jargon that we didn't understand but certain phrases caught my eye…

Purchase land… bulldoze castle… drill prime gas reserves…

"What does it mean?" asked Connor, also inspecting the papers.

I shook my head. "I'm not sure." Although I didn't understand most of it, I could see that *Frank I.C.G.* wanted to extend their drilling operation into the grounds of Glenkilly Castle and the phrase *'bulldoze castle'* showed precisely what they intended to do.

Suddenly, the door on the opposite side of the room burst open – almost tearing from its hinges as it clattered against the wall – and the tall, growling guard with the crooked teeth and the greying, messy hair crashed into the room, his eyes red with fury.

CHAPTER FORTY-ONE: BRAVE

The guard glared down at me like an eagle that had found a fox eating eggs in its nest. His angry, bloodshot eyes flashed from me to Connor and then to the papers in my hand.

"Hey! You can't touch those!"

He spat out the words before lunging at us. We dodged, banging against the wall. Darting away, the guard came after me. Connor shoved him in the back, almost toppling him over. He spun, swinging a fist, but luckily missed Connor by some distance.

Like a Formula One car whizzing around the track, I circled the guard, sending him dizzy. He grabbed at me but I dodged again. Connor and I barged through the nearest door, zooming away from the cabin before the guard got near.

Outside, our feet pounded the wet ground and my pulse throbbed in my ears. As we raced together into the pitch-black woods, I heard the guard's raspy breath and clumping footsteps behind us. Zigzagging between the trees, we managed to keep the man a good distance behind us.

Daniel Henshaw

Thankfully, we were swifter, more agile and could squeeze through the tight spaces between bushes and shrubs, whereas the guard was huge and lumbering and his big, round beer-belly suggested that he was more than a few pounds overweight. It was like an elephant trying to catch two mice. Still, we weren't going to risk slowing down and it certainly wasn't easy – with the mud and the sludge and the slimy moss. We were sprinting, slipping and sliding through the woods, fuelled by pure adrenaline.

With low branches clawing at our faces and prickly brambles trying to trip us, I had a sudden brainwave. Once we'd hurdled a fallen log, putting ourselves a good thirty metres ahead of the guard, I stopped. Grabbing Connor by the arm, I pulled him to crouch behind the thickest tree trunk nearby. We remained absolutely still. Didn't breathe. Didn't move. Just listened.

"Where've those piggin' brats gone?" the guard hissed beneath his breath. "I'm gonna need the dogs." He trudged on, struggling through the dense, tangled undergrowth, right past our hiding place, into the deep, dark, gloom of the forest.

We waited a few minutes, expecting him to return. Still we didn't move. But no more footsteps came, just the spray of rain and a rustle of leaves above.

Slowly, carefully, we rose to our feet, breathing as quietly as possible. We crept away from the big trunk and turned back towards the drilling site, where we'd left Nazirah and Michael. Had they escaped? Which direction would they have gone?

I then realised I still had the papers from the cabin gripped in my hand. The top sheet was a black and white map. It showed the grounds of Glenkilly Castle and *Frank I.C.G.* from above. When I passed the map to Connor, he was staring at me with a star-struck gaze, as if I'd transformed into a Premier League footballer or the lead singer of his favourite rock band.

"What?" I said.

"You saved me." Connor's sopping black fringe was plastered to his forehead. "Thanks, Jeremy. Thank you so much."

I shrugged. "It was all *my* fault anyway. I tricked you… into thinking I'd seen Zach."

"Yeah, well, let's forget about that," said Connor.

But I didn't want to forget. I immediately became defensive. "I only did it for payback! You scared me and made me jump into that soaking bush! Why do you hate me so much?"

"Hate you? What are you on about?"

"You embarrass me in front of everyone, you call me 'Jellyfish', and now you want to take Michael from me."

Connor laughed, shaking his head. "It's just that... well, you don't really care, do you?"

I frowned. "Care? What do you mean?"

"You don't care that you're terrible at everything. You don't care that you can't play football... or do maths... or shoot a bow and arrow. And yet... *everyone loves Jeremy*. Michael adores you, for some reason, and so does Nazirah. Who do I have? Who likes me?"

This made me stop and think. Who *were* Connor's friends? He might make people laugh when he mocked me but nobody really hung around with him. I thought back to playtimes at school and couldn't remember seeing him having fun with friends. I just couldn't picture it.

"Is that what you really think?" I said. "That I don't care? I *hate* being weak. I *hate* being scared of everything."

"Well, you don't look scared to me," said Connor.

"What do you mean?"

"Well, you're here... in the dark... in the middle of these woods... and you just rescued me from a crazy man. You look pretty brave to me, Jeremy."

I glanced around at the shadows. Huge black trees surrounded us like silent spies. Rain continued to trickle through

254

the leaves. But all was still. For now, we were safe. And for the first time… I realised… it was because of me. I'd saved Connor. I'd found this safe spot. I'd been… *brave*.

"Sorry," Connor said after a long pause. "I didn't know you were so scared. And I didn't know the things I said upset you so much."

I smiled. "I'm sorry too. I should *not* have told you that I'd seen your cousin."

"And I shouldn't have made you jump into a bush. And I promise not to call you 'Jellyfish' anymore."

"Thanks." I stepped towards him, bent my elbow and pointed it towards him. Connor grinned, brushed his wet fringe aside and then bumped my elbow.

"Now," I said with a renewed sense of determination, "where *is* Michael?"

CHAPTER FORTY-TWO: B.O. AND FAGS

It felt good to have cleared the air with Connor.

Nazirah had been right. Talking about our problems had helped. And to think, he was actually envious of *me!* He thought that I was popular and laid-back, not caring about my constant failures. How wrong he'd been! I guess you never know what's going on inside someone else's head.

Shivering against the cold wind, my teeth chattering, I looked at Connor, his hair drenched and clothes splattered with mud. We must've looked like a pair of drowned rats. Rain continued to trickle through the leaves, slithering down trunks and soaking the ground. The damp scent of wet soil almost covered up the foul, gassy smell of the fracking operation. Almost.

"Do you know where Michael is?" I asked, a feeling of dread creeping up on me.

Connor wiped the dripping hair from his forehead. "I don't know. They put us in different rooms."

"Keep your voice down," I whispered.

The ferocious guard was still out here somewhere and would soon have those scary, hairy dogs with their sharp sense of smell and even sharper teeth! And, of course, there was Maureen. What had happened to the creature? Hadn't it entered the cabin where Connor had been? Did that mean that the security guard was the monster? If so, why didn't he transform into the beast just now?

"Who grabbed you?" I eventually asked.

Connor's eyes filled with fear. "The Wendigo. It grabbed us both."

I nodded. That's what I'd thought. "But… the guard said *'The Boss'* brought you in."

Connor frowned. "I know. I didn't get that. The beast grabbed us and took us to the cabin. It threw me into that room. I don't know where it took Michael. I thought I was gonna die. Then, a few minutes later, that security guard came in and tied me up."

"So you think the guard is the Wendigo? That he transforms? Like a shape-shifter?"

Connor shook his head. "No. Here's the weird thing. The security guard… he stank. He smelled of B.O. and fags. The monster didn't."

"The monster didn't smell?"

"Well, it didn't smell of *those* things. It smelled... nice. Like perfume. Flowery perfume."

My mind flashed back to the dead rabbits and the abandoned farm. In places I'd seen the creature, the smell of perfume had lingered... a scent of jasmine.

"Did the monster speak?" I asked.

Connor shook his head. "It didn't make any noises. No growling. Nothing."

"Did you hear any other voices in the cabin?"

"No. Just the security guard."

"And you didn't see Zach?"

Connor scowled. "You don't still think Zach is involved?"

"No. I just wondered if he was there. You didn't see him?"

"No!" Connor's eyes had become wide and fierce as if to underline the point that Zach had nothing to do with this business.

He then held up the sheets of paper that I'd snatched from the porta-cabin. "These papers must be worth something because that bloke didn't want us to have them."

I nodded but didn't answer. I had more questions about the cabin but I didn't get chance to ask them because I suddenly realised... we were being watched.

CHAPTER FORTY-THREE: THE CHASE

We tried to hide, tucking ourselves into the middle of a bush, branches scraping our faces, rain dripping, bums soggy against the damp ground.

Closing my eyes, I gripped Connor's arm and thought of my beautiful, strong mum, wishing she were here now to protect me, to stroke my hair and tell me everything would be alright. I wished I'd never agreed to come on this stupid trip, to this god-forsaken, haunted place.

The dark figure was nearby now, looming above us with its huge antlered head and humanlike body. Could it see us? Sense us? Smell us?

An enormous branch had fallen from a tree, blocking our path to one side. The beast approached from the other direction and thick, tangled brush surrounded us on all sides. We were trapped.

I whimpered.

And the creature must have heard me because its head tilted towards us.

This was it.

The monster was going to kill us.

And for what? What had we ever done?

Well, we'd cut a big hole in a fence, broken onto *Frank I.C.G.* property and stolen some important papers.

But apart from all of that… what had we *ever* done?

The Wendigo crept closer. My heart punched at my ribs like an angry boxer. Connor yelped as the creature lurched, grabbing with its claws.

Luckily, a harsh wind then swirled, shifting a low-hanging branch and revealing another footpath.

Another way out!

Yanking Connor's arm, I heaved us from the bush. We darted, our feet squelching, slipping, stumbling. The monster squealed as we raced past.

Unsure where to go, we ran ahead. Hurtling through bushes; thorns and branches scraped our skin. My pulse pounded in my ears. Somewhere behind us, the Wendigo bashed its way through the woods, continuing the chase.

Tumbling into the moonlight, the filthy pond stood before us. Somehow, charging through the darkness of the forest, we'd circled the pond. The guard's cabin – Connor's former prison –

was now beyond the water. I glanced through the mist but saw no sign of Nazirah or Michael. We began to sprint back towards the little cabin. Maybe we could find our friends. Maybe we could find Zach. Maybe we could find someone, anyone to help us.

But the moment we moved in the direction of the cabin, the beast reappeared, crashing through the trees, saliva dripping from its mouth. Sharp antlers sprouted from the creature's cheeks like a tangle of Samurai swords.

Spinning on our heels, we turned away.

But where could we go?

Back into the forest? No way! The ground was too uneven and slippy. We could barely see in the pitch dark, fighting our way through the bracken and tangled undergrowth. It would only be a matter of time before Maureen caught us.

My eyes flashed in every direction, desperate to see something. An escape route, a place to hide, anything.

And then I saw it. Why had I been so blind? It had been there all along. The drilling rig! Looming over us like a giant metal maze, the drilling rig climbed towards the night sky like an enormous, hollow skeleton of thin, metallic bones.

As I gazed up at the huge structure, I was reminded of the rocket launches done by NASA. There were always these cage-like towers next to the rockets before they blasted into the sky.

The drilling rig appeared to be made only of metal bars and I could see right through it. An uncountable number stairs zigzagged their way to the top and, as I arched my neck, gazing up at the enormous tower, I thought of a skyscraper… like the ones in New York. And I wondered if there was a thirteenth floor.

Thirteen. Unlucky for some.

We raced towards the drilling rig. Maybe there'd be somewhere to hide. Maybe we could lose the creature in there, just like in a real maze.

The monster screamed as it gave chase.

A set of metal stairs stood at the side of the tower. And at the top of these stairs was an entrance, an open metal doorframe. The entrance was narrow and low. It gave me an idea.

We closed in on the metal steps.

But Maureen was catching up.

One last surge of speed.

Ten metres to the stairs. Maureen just behind.

My arms pumped with every last ounce of power.

Five metres.

Three.

Maureen grabbed.

One metre.

We charged up the steps, our feet clanging on the metal.

My thighs ached. Maureen was just behind.

As we approached the open doorframe at the top of the stairs, the creature's claws grasped hold of my coat just before we tumbled through the drilling rig's entrance.

The monster's huge head and antlers banged against the doorframe, stopping it from entering. Its grip released my coat, sending me flying through the gap, onto the metal floor, landing with a loud clunk.

Catching our breath, we lay sprawled on the ground at the foot of another staircase, safely inside the huge metal tower. Puffing and panting, I wanted to vomit.

"HA!" Connor yelled, his breathless voice echoing around the hollow structure. "Can't get us now, can you? Stupid animal!" He stood up and began bouncing around, throwing air-punches like a boxer before a fight. The sheets of paper we'd stolen from the cabin were still in his hand.

Outside the entrance, the Wendigo watched us with emotionless red eyes. Clouds of steam blasted from its nostrils. The monster's head tilted, trying to solve the puzzle.

Then, sickness lurched in my throat as I realised what it was doing.

The creature tilted its head further, poking one set of antlers through the doorframe. It shifted its head, pulling the antlers through the space. It was smarter than we'd thought!

"It's coming through!" Connor yelled.

With nowhere else to turn, we charged to the steps and began our ascent up the enormous tower.

Because that was definitely the safest place to be... right?

CHAPTER FORTY-FOUR: CERTAIN DEATH

Metal stairs clanked beneath our feet. Up and up, round and round, in a dizzying spiral we went, climbing up the staircase at the side of the drilling rig. Maureen was now inside, pounding the steel steps below us. Wind rattled the scaffolded tower, almost shaking us off balance. Higher we scrambled, leaping three steps at a time. The clunk of our footsteps echoed down the tower shaft.

The stairs then opened out into a bare landing, an open space. To our left, the gaps between the scaffolding of thick metal bars allowed the wind and rain to swirl in. To our right, a banister. Over its edge, a gigantic drop fell towards a black hole going deep, deep, deep down into the crust of the Earth.

Then we saw the door.

Leading where? Higher? Back down?

We tried the handle.

Locked.

We pushed and banged and rattled and kicked. But the door wouldn't budge. We were trapped.

The only other exit was back down the stairs. But as the clang of footsteps echoed up, we knew it wasn't an option. Maureen was coming. The footsteps slowed as the antlers began to appear from the stairs below.

My knees shook in terror. Fear pulsed through every vein. The monster stepped higher, taking each step with caution and care. It had no intention of letting us leave. Its head appeared above the horizon of the top step, its fur dripping wet with rain and saliva, clouds of hot breath escaping its nostrils. Its great black torso came into view and then its sharp claws.

I banged my back against the locked door, hoping it would crash open. But it barely budged.

As the beast stepped onto the landing area, its feet made an almighty *THUD* against the floor. It breathed heavily, croakily, like a dragon ready to release a great blast of fire from deep within its chest. Stepping with slow, meaningful movements, the creature ignored me, heading straight towards Connor, who stood with his back against the thin metal banister, just a pole of metal between him and an epic fall into a pit of darkness below. A fall of certain death.

The Wendigo stepped closer to Connor, swiping with a vicious claw. Connor flinched, jerking backwards, almost falling.

Connor told me I was brave.

I *was* brave.

And now was the time to prove it.

"Hey!" I yelled, inching away from the door. "Leave him alone!" The monster ignored me, towering over Connor. Bravely (or stupidly), I lunged at the beast's arm, grabbing its elbow. Maureen flung me to one side like it had swatted a fly. My bottom hit the ground hard.

Then, as a gust of wind rattled the tower, a familiar smell met my nostrils. The sweet scent of jasmine... just like when I first saw the creature by the dead rabbits and again at the farmhouse.

I looked up to see Maureen, pushing at Connor's chest, trying to prize the *Frank I.C.G.* papers from his hand. I glanced at the creature's feet. The trainers. Black Reebok trainers.

And then my brain went into overdrive.

I thought of Nazirah's words.

It's a woodland beast. Why is it even wearing trainers?

I thought of the *Frank I.C.G.* papers. Why would a monster from a legendary curse need to take those papers from a ten-year-old boy?

I thought of the guard's words: *The Boss didn't bring you in here for no piggin' reason!*

I thought of the I.D. card. The person working at both *Frank I.C.G.* and Glenkilly Castle.

I thought of contact lenses… and who might wear them.

I thought of the scent. Jasmine. Exotic flowers. And I recalled where I'd first smelled it.

And then, I finally understood what was going on.

CHAPTER FORTY-FIVE: DISASTER PLAN

The monster continued its attempts to wrestle the papers from Connor's hands. Connor's feet half-stepped over the edge of the landing. Maureen's other arm pressed his body into the metal bar, almost pushing him through the gap.

If I didn't do something now, he was going to fall.

"Stop it!" I yelled. "Stop it, Kat! Or should I call you Natasha?"

The monster, who'd been all snarls and grunts and wildly thrashing arms, froze when it heard the name on the I.D. card. The creature took half a step away from Connor before turning my way. An icy wind swept across the landing, bringing a flurry of raindrops through the gaps in the scaffolding.

"I know it's you under there, Kat. You don't need to pretend anymore."

The monster growled again – but half-heartedly this time. It took a step towards me but I held my ground. I thought I heard something bang on the stairs below but assumed it must have been the wind.

"I know what's been going on, Kat. You've been under that costume all along. I can smell your perfume. And I can see your Reeboks. I know that you're in charge over here. I know that you're The Boss. Is Natasha your real name?"

The creature didn't move.

I went on. "We've read the plans of your company. You want to take over the land owned by Glenkilly Castle. You've been scaring kids away with your tale about a monster living in the grounds."

The Wendigo stepped menacingly towards me. Silent. Threatening. It stood as tall and aggressive as ever. Fear stabbed at my gut. We had nowhere to run.

But then… slowly… like a bouncy castle being deflated, the creature's shoulders sagged. It gave out a great sigh as it reached up to grip the antlers protruding from its cheeks. The monster lifted the massive head away from its own shoulders, revealing a much smaller head beneath.

Kat's face was an odd mix of failure and anger, her red hair sweaty and tangled. She held the fake head with great care, as if handling the crown jewels.

Then she laughed. It was an ugly laugh. But now I knew the truth. Inside, she was an ugly person.

"You think you know everything, do you?" she sneered.

I shook my head. "I don't know the capital of Moldova."

"But you know about our plan? Our great Master Plan?"

Another howl of wind rattled the tower. I shivered.

Then, out the corner of my eye, I saw movement on the stairs. Perhaps it was nothing. Perhaps it was just the moonlight shifting shadows. Perhaps my tired mind had started imagining things.

"I've only worked out the basics," I admitted. "*Frank I.C.G.* wants to buy Glenkilly Castle, knock it down and drill through it."

Kat/Natasha nodded, screwing her face up into a grisly grimace, as if she were smelling the gassy stench of the river for the first time.

"You see, this area of Scotland is… pointless. It's nothing but trees and fields and on the three days of the year when the sun actually appears, swarms of midges arrive to bite every inch of your skin, like little flying vampires." She sniggered. "Glenkilly is a wasteland. There's nothing here. But we're about to change that – with the greatest innovation the world has ever seen."

I frowned. "You mean one of the pens with invisible ink?"

271

"No! Fracking. Fracking is the future. It's going to save the world. Cheap energy from right under our feet, just waiting to be released. And where's the richest source of natural gas in the UK? Right beneath Glenkilly Castle. We just need to get rid of that ugly building and we can start drilling. Get rid of all this useless countryside, wasting acres and acres of space."

"The countryside's beautiful," I said. "The landscape is stunning. And animals live here."

"Animals? This is more important than animals. This is about humans, and humans depend on machines now. And machines need to be powered. The coal has all been mined and oil levels are running low. We need new sources of energy. We need this gas. The existence of humans as a species depends on it."

"But there has to be another way," I said. "You've contaminated the water and poisoned the air and knocked down hundreds of trees. Animals are dying! You can't just go around destroying beautiful places. What's the point in humans existing if there's no beauty left for us to enjoy?"

Kat grunted. "We just need to knock down that castle."

"The castle has been here for hundreds of years. It's a great place for kids."

Kat cackled like an old, red-headed witch. "*That* castle? That one castle in the middle of nowhere, with nothing else around? That castle is like an ugly zit on the immaculate face of natural gas. That castle is the only obstacle to creating a new Scotland, a richer Scotland, a Scotland that will be the envy of the world. And now we're close to succeeding, so very close."

"You see," she went on, "we've known how valuable this land is for a long time. But the Scottish government refuses to sell it because the castle has its history. And it brings them a steady income, with snivelling children rolling in to hike and canoe and try to make it through the night without wetting their pants."

A nasty snarl had appeared on her face.

Master Plan? This was more like a Disaster Plan.

My eyes flicked to the edge of the staircase again. I spotted a dark figure move through the blackest of the shadows, silently creeping up the stairs.

And that's when I knew. Somebody else was here.

CHAPTER FORTY-SIX: END OF THE LINE

Kat looked ridiculous, in her strange gorilla outfit and Reebok trainers, as if she were hosting a weird fancy dress party at the top of a freezing cold tower at half past two in the morning.

Connor had edged away from the danger of the banister, and the deadly hundred-metre drop, and was now standing by my side. Kat didn't seem to notice him. She didn't seem to care about him anymore. She had her story to tell and she wanted somebody – anybody – to hear it.

The mystery figure remained on the stairwell shadows, silent and still. To avoid exposing them, I kept my eyes totally focused on Kat as she continued talking.

"To buy the land, we increased our offer again and again but still the government wouldn't sell the damned castle. We had to come up with a plan, a Master Plan so to speak: Get rid of the stupid kids, make Glenkilly Castle worthless."

"So what," Connor interrupted, "you dressed up as a monster and scared all the kids away?"

Kat smirked. "Precisely. We invented a tale, a legend. *The Glenkilly Curse*. You may have heard about it. A great big monster stalking the land because of a selfish duke who built the castle on a burial ground."

"Yeah," I said. "Zach told us."

"Ah, Zach," Kat smiled, with a hint of pride. "We had the myth. We had the costume. All we needed then was a gullible fool who believed in ghosts and ghouls enough to come and work here and tell the story of Maureen to every child. Zach was the perfect candidate."

Her grin became demonic as she revelled in the memories. "A few sightings of the monster in the woods, a handful of kids go missing in the night and teachers are panicking all over the place. Well, you know what *parents* can be like, they complain to school if their kid goes home with the wrong cardigan or they get a sniffle because they played tennis in the rain for five minutes. Imagine if the class returned to school without their child at all. Oh, the teachers were absolutely losing their minds with worry."

Kat laughed, staring into space as she recalled a distant memory. I glanced at the stairwell. Although the dark figure was no longer moving, I noticed a faint glow. A mobile phone?

"You see," Kat continued, snapping my attention back to her, "most schools couldn't even last a few days, their kids were so scared. They demanded refunds. And then they went home, telling other teachers from other schools about the horrors of Glenkilly Castle. And those teachers tell others. The newspapers were all over it too. Word soon spread. *Avoid Glenkilly Castle.* Bookings dried up. Nobody wanted to come here anymore. The place went from having eight, nine, ten schools here a week – each with forty, fifty, a hundred kids, all paying a fortune to stay – down to three bookings a week, then two, and then your school, the only visitors this month."

Kat paused to sigh before producing another ugly smile.

"Glenkilly Castle can barely pay its bills. Its reputation is in the gutter. Zero bookings for the rest of the year. Once your teacher realises that you're missing too, there'll be demands for refunds. Glenkilly will be out of business. Now the bulldozers can move in and the drilling will begin."

Her eyes then hardened as she glared at us.

"But now I have problem, don't I? What should I do with you two little pests?" She glanced towards the banister and the never-ending drop. "Do you know how deep that hole is? It goes

276

way, way down into the centre of the Earth. It'd be extremely difficult to find anyone who might have *'fallen'* down there."

My chest tightened.

"Is that –" I hesitated before finishing my question, scared of the answer. "Is that what you did with Michael?"

Kat frowned. "Michael?"

"Yes. My best friend. You grabbed him in the woods."

"When you captured me too," said Connor.

Kat sneered. "Oh, that little nuisance." She glanced at the drop once more. "He's in a better place now."

"Disney Land?" said Connor.

Kat smirked. "I'm afraid that your friend has finally… *reached the end of the line.*"

I felt my insides collapse inside me.

She'd killed him!

She'd killed my best friend!

Thrown him into the hole, never to be seen again.

I heard myself whimper.

Michael was dead. And it was all *my fault*! I'd played the prank on Connor. And Michael had joined him. He'd been captured by this evil witch and now he was dead!

Tears rolled down my cheek. I moaned, a high-pitched shriek, like an injured fox.

But I didn't have time to mourn.

Kat suddenly leapt towards us, the sharp claws of her costume pointed at our faces.

We ducked and rolled, out of her grasp. She wanted to kill *us* too! We knew the truth and she had to keep us silent.

Her head flashed our way.

We scampered for the stairs.

Kat charged.

Then came a voice from the stairwell.

"That's enough, Kat!" Zach yelled as he stepped onto the landing.

Kat halted, her eyes filled with shock. "No! Impossible! How did you get here? You were locked in the boiler room."

Swift as a snake, Zach was by my side, shoving a mobile phone into my hand. "Take this. I recorded everything. The police are on their way. Run!"

Grabbing the phone, I darted down the stairs, taking them three at a time, Connor hurtling after me. Our feet clanged against the metal steps. Behind us, I heard Kat scream. Zach shouted something at her but we never turned back. As we bounded down the stairs, I saw blue flashing lights through the darkness of the trees.

CHAPTER FORTY-SEVEN: WORST NIGHT EVER

When we reached the bottom of the stairs, sploshing onto the wet grass, my legs gave way – like jelly – and I collapsed in a heap on the muddy ground.

Jellyfish don't have bones.

I felt my face crumple and my lips quiver. Saliva ran from my mouth as every bottled-up emotion poured from my body. I wailed, tears flooding from my eyes. My shoulders and chest jerked violently.

Michael was *dead*.

My hands shook. The nerves in my body had tightened like wires. Sickness swirled in my gut.

She *killed* him!

Two police cars pulled up near the cabin across the dirty pond, blue lights twirling. Four uniformed officers approached, running around the water's edge, their feet squelching. They said something, though I didn't hear what through my sobs.

I held up the mobile phone for them to listen to and, in between tears, I yelled, "She killed my best friend! She pushed him down the hole!"

As Connor explained everything, a fifth person arrived. A man in a long raincoat introduced himself as Detective Stevenson. He appeared to be in charge. He had ginger hair and a thick moustache filling half of his face. He reminded me of a walrus.

Stevenson sent three of the uniformed officers up the stairs before asking the fourth to take Connor and me to the patrol car. After a few tense minutes, watching the tower through a thousand tears, I eventually saw Kat being dragged down in handcuffs by two police officers. Her face was red and flustered, her eyes wide and bewildered. The dark, hairy Wendigo costume still covered the rest of her body.

Zach appeared moments later with a female officer. Thankfully, he hadn't been arrested.

Kat was squeezed into one patrol car, while Connor, Zach and I were taken back to Glenkilly Castle in another. All I recall of the journey was the rain, hammering against the car's roof like a million bullets. If any of us spoke, I don't remember what was said. I could only think of one thing… the pain. The pain of losing Michael.

*

Back at the castle, we found Nazirah with Mr Hopton and Mrs Dodd. The teachers looked gaunt and pale, as if they'd just seen a hundred ghosts. Connor explained what had happened in the tower. Everyone cried out in shock.

Detective Stevenson, along with a female officer, whose name I don't recall, took us into the dining hall, where they spoke to us individually about what had happened. They made notes and thanked us for helping before saying that we could finally go to bed. 03:43, according to my watch. The latest I'd ever stay up… and my worst night ever.

Just as I was about to make my way up to bed, Detective Stevenson tapped me on the shoulder.

"That was great work in the tower," he said softly. "I've listened to the recording. The way you worked out what had been going on… that's the sign of a true detective. You should certainly consider a career in the police force when you're older."

I half-nodded, half-shrugged and then fully yawned. I was too tired to think about my future. I just wanted to sleep. But I knew that – with the loss of Michael heavy on my heart – sleep would be far from easy.

FRIDAY

CHAPTER FORTY-EIGHT: ONE FINAL CLUE

I didn't sleep. Not at all.

When I eventually went back downstairs, I felt like a zombie, sleepwalking through the castle. Mr Hopton was waiting in the dining hall. He looked like he'd aged fifty years over the course of the week, which was saying something because he must have been fifty to begin with!

Glancing at the antique clock on the mantelpiece, I saw the time was just after eight. I assume this meant eight in the morning as it was light outside and Nazirah was at one of the tables, nibbling some toast. Connor and Zach huddled opposite her, not eating, just embracing each other. All the other children were stuck in the Games Room while everything was being sorted.

I sat next to Nazirah but refused to eat. My mouth was drier than a camel's back, and my teeth felt just as furry. Greedily glugging a glass of orange juice, I stared into space, vacant, not speaking. The silence of the castle wrapped itself around me, like a giant bubble. I was so numb, someone could have poked me with a sharp needle and I wouldn't have noticed. Nothing felt real.

Memories of Michael reeled through my head as I sat there. The made up stories; owning a pet buffalo named Brian and a genie who could only speak Mongolian and a Bible signed by Jesus. I half-smiled at the memories while half-listening to Zach as he explained how he'd been imprisoned at *Frank I.C.G.*

"It was the night we went to the farm," he began. He told us how he went for a wee behind the farmhouse and when he came back, he saw the Wendigo chasing me. He followed at a good speed but the creature soon stopped, leaving me to go careering through the woods, all the way back to Glenkilly Castle. Zach continued to watch the monster as it paused, turned and then returned to *Frank I.C.G.*

Zach said he knew of a secret gap in the fence and after squeezing through it, he managed to keep up with the beast, observing it through the trees. He watched it go into the cabin and take off its costume and was then utterly shocked to see his workmate Kat underneath.

Once she left the cabin, Zach broke in and saw the plans for the drilling and the plot to bulldoze Glenkilly Castle. Zach was making photocopies of the papers when something hard cracked him around the head. The next thing he knew, he was locked up in a dark room.

Nazirah then chipped in with her side of the story. After the guard had chased me and Connor, she'd snuck into the cabin and found Zach in one of the adjoining rooms. After releasing him, Nazirah rushed back to the castle while Zach headed for the drilling rig. Zach managed to record Kat bragging about her 'Master Plan' just in time.

Interrupting us, Detective Stevenson then entered the dining hall and asked to speak to the cousins again. Zach and Connor stood up and left the room, along with Mr Hopton who'd been busy all morning making phone calls to school and parents. I wondered if he'd rung Michael's mum yet. It would destroy her. I felt tears welling up once more. A hard, thick lump formed in my throat. My mouth dried out.

I sat in silence, trying not to sob.

Then Nazirah spoke. "What did she say?"

It took a moment for the words to soak into my ruined brain. I slowly turned to look at Nazirah. "Sorry?"

She put down her fork. "Kat, Natasha, whatever her name is. What did she say? At the top of the tower. What did she say about Michael? Exactly."

I shook my head. "I'm trying not to think about it. But it's impossible. It keeps playing over and over again. Like a recurring nightmare."

A long silence passed by.

"Do you think she's really capable of killing someone?" Nazirah eventually asked.

I frowned. "Capable? She *did* kill someone! And she wanted to kill me too." Tears were forming again.

"But what if she didn't? What if it was an empty threat?"

"What do you mean?"

"Connor told me all about her Master Plan to scare people away from Glenkilly Castle. *Scaring* is the key here. I don't think she – or anyone at *Frank I.C.G.* – would go as far as actually killing someone, especially not a child."

"What exactly are you saying, Nazirah?"

"Tell me what Kat said at the top of the tower. About Michael."

I thought for a moment, replaying every second in my mind, like I was watching the scariest horror movie of all time. I tried to remember each word precisely.

"I asked her what she'd done with Michael. At first, she didn't know who I was talking about. Then we mentioned him being grabbed in the woods. She called him *'a little nuisance'* and then said that he'd *'finally reached the end of the line'*."

Nazirah rubbed her chin. "And that's it?"

I nodded. "She didn't say anything else about Michael, I don't think. But she threatened us, saying that nobody would find us if we fell down the hole."

"But she didn't *actually* say that she'd killed him?"

"She suggested it."

"But, Jeremy, don't you see? Kat admitted *everything* to you. All of her plans, the way they'd ruined the castle's reputation, why they wanted the land, even the fact that they'd hired Zach specifically to scare people. She told you *everything*, very clearly."

"I know. I was there."

"But she never *actually* said that she'd pushed Michael into the hole. She just hinted at it. I think she may have been leaving you one final clue."

My breathing suddenly tightened. Hope sprung into my heart. My belly rolled with nerves.

"So, what are you saying?" I asked. "That Michael's still alive?"

Nazirah nodded. "Precisely."

CHAPTER FORTY-NINE: ENORMOUS WASHING LINE

I'm afraid that your friend has finally… reached the end of the line.

The words played over and over in my mind.

If this was a clue, what did it mean?

Finally reached the end of the line.

I felt like I'd heard the words somewhere before.

End of the line.

"Where might there be a *line*?" I asked Nazirah. We remained seated in the dining hall.

She rubbed her chin. "You could draw a line. Maybe on paper or in the sand."

"But how would that relate to Michael? There isn't any sand here."

"What about soil?" she said. "Is there anywhere that has a big line in the soil? Or any lines marked somewhere on the grass?"

Nowhere sprang to mind. "They have some football goals in the field over there." I pointed in the vague direction of the fields. "But there's no pitch marked out. No lines or anything."

Nazirah sighed. "Mr Hopton taught us about *line* graphs in maths this year – but I can't see how that's relevant."

"What about the lines in Mr Hopton's face? You know, his wrinkles."

"How could they be a clue?"

I shrugged.

"What about a fishing rod?" Nazirah suggested. "A rod has a line. Do they do fishing here?"

I shrugged again. "No idea."

"Could Michael be at the bottom of some water? At the end of a fishing line?"

"I hope not," I answered. "Because that still means he's…"

"Okay, okay." Nazirah held up her hands, seeing me get upset again. "Let's park the fishing line idea to one side. What other kinds of lines do we know?"

"Railway line?"

Nazirah shook her head. "There's no railway near here, I'm sure of it."

"Lines in a play?"

"Has Michael been in a play?"

I thought for a moment. "He once told me he'd played Macbeth in Stratford-Upon-Avon… but I'm pretty sure that wasn't true."

We sat in silence for a moment.

"Don't we queue in a line?" said Nazirah.

I nodded. "Queueing for dinner?" Our eyes flashed around the dining hall. "Could the next clue be here?" I saw nothing out of the ordinary. Same stags' heads and ugly portraits of old men on the wall. High ceiling, tartan carpet, tables, chairs. Nothing new.

"How about the queues to the activities?" asked Nazirah.

"Maybe. We queued ages for the Go-Karts. But how would that relate to Michael?"

Nazirah frowned. "Was Michael particularly good at the Go-Karts?"

"Not especially."

"Were there any activities he was brilliant at? Or terrible?"

I thought quietly for a bit, trying to remember each activity, trying to push the flashbacks of the previous night away.

Nazirah continued firing questions, her mind constantly churning out ideas.

"What about a washing line? Has Michael done any washing while he's been here?"

And then it hit me.

Not a washing line as such, but very similar. Something that ran from one tree, through the top of the forest, ending at another tree in the distance. Something Michael was terrible at. He was the one person who didn't reach the end of the line.

I'm afraid that your friend has finally… reached the end of the line.

My heart almost bounced through my ribcage.

Without any explanation, I stood up and raced for the door.

"Everybody follow me!"

*

"Jeremy, why are we here?"

Mr Hopton had chased me through the woods, along with Detective Stevenson and Nazirah.

"You shouldn't really be here," Detective Stevenson added. "This is a potential crime scene."

"I think you may be right," I said, staring up to the top of the trees. To our right, stood the huge Scots pine tree with steps winding around it, leading to the start of the zip-line. My eyes followed the thick, black cable that ran through the treetops… like an enormous *washing line*. I looked along the cable, right to the point where everybody (except Michael) bumped against the opposite platform… *the end of the line.*

And that's when I saw it.

Right at the end of the zip-line, hung a huge black rucksack, a camping bag, the sort used by serious hikers. And it was just hanging there on the line, like a pair of washed knickers pegged out to dry. Well, apart from the fact that the bag was… moving, ever-so-slightly. Wriggling.

"Jeremy, why are we here?" Mr Hopton repeated.

I pointed at the black rucksack. "Michael!"

Everyone's eyes shifted to the sky.

"Holy smokes!" Detective Stevenson gasped in a thick Scottish accent, before charging towards the second pine tree, the finishing post. Mr Hopton followed.

Nazirah's mouth had opened into a giant O. She looked totally shocked. In fact, for a moment, she looked just as stupid as the rest of us.

"I don't believe it," she said. "It *was* a final clue. I was right."

"Of course you were right," I replied, gently placing a hand on Nazirah's arm. "You're always right."

She shook her head. "I didn't actually believe it, though. I was only saying it to make you feel better... to give you some hope, something to focus on instead of your sadness."

"Oh great, thanks!" I said with half a smile.

We watched in silence as Detective Stevenson and Mr Hopton arrived on the platform above.

"Should we be wearing hard hats up here?" I heard Mr Hopton say.

Detective Stevenson grabbed the long pole with the hook on the end. "If we fall from here," he said, "a hard hat won't save us."

He reached out with the pole, hooked the harnesses holding the rucksack and heaved the weight towards him. He wobbled a little and, for a split-second, I panicked that he may actually fall. But he managed to steady himself. Mr Hopton helped drag the heavy bag onto the platform and they quickly unzipped it.

With my eyes glued to the scene, my insides felt like they'd collapsed and my knees suddenly gave way. I fell to the floor as I watched Michael step out of the rucksack and onto the platform.

He looked dazed, confused and terrified. But, more importantly than any of that… he looked… *alive!*

CHAPTER FIFTY: HOOVES... AND ANTLERS?

"So, she just told you everything?" Michael asked.

I nodded, sitting in my seat, ready for the coach-ride home. Once again, I was cramped uncomfortably between the window and Michael. He'd taken the aisle seat *again*, *still* claiming to have his ridiculous window allergy.

"It was like she wanted to show off," I said. *"Look at all the things I've done.* She probably thought she could say it to a pair of kids and get away with it. Who were we going to tell? Who'd believe us anyway?"

The coach driver turned the ignition and the engine rumbled into action. Above our heads, the air conditioning vents kicked in.

"Do you think she would've pushed you into the hole?" Michael asked.

I shrugged. "Who knows? She's clearly nuts. You'd have to be pretty crazy to go around dressing up as a monster to put an ancient castle out of business."

Michael laughed, shaking his head. "And Zach was recording the whole thing?"

"Yep. Nicked that guard's phone and got the whole thing recorded. Detective Stevenson says that Kat will be sent to prison for a long time."

"What are they charging her with?"

"Loads of stuff," I said. "Kidnapping, fraud, running an illegal fracking operation and some environmental crimes too. And that guard was arrested."

A wave of concern washed over Michael's face. "So… if the legend of the curse and the demons was all made up, how did the river set on fire? Y'know, if it's not actually a passage to Hell? And who's been killing all the animals?"

"It was all to do with the fracking," I replied, trying to sound smart. "Nazirah explained it to me. When they blast the gas from the Earth, loads of it gets into the water. So, it made the river flammable. And the animals were dying because of it too. They were drinking the water and breathing it in and it made them sick, with their fur falling out and some of them dying. That part of Zach's story was true… it just had nothing to do with phone lines. It was all because of the fracking."

Michael nodded slowly, starting to relax after being shaken by the whole kidnapping experience… and then hung from a zip-line for eight hours. And no, I hadn't *made* him sit with me on the coach, he'd chosen to sit here.

"I'm so sorry," I suddenly blurted.

Michael's forehead creased. "Sorry about what?"

"Everything!"

"You don't need to be sorry. You solved the case. You worked out that Kat was behind it all. And then you found me. *The end of the line.* Brilliant. That was just like the clue I solved when I was working a police case with –"

"But it was all my fault! I sent you and Connor into the woods, pretending I'd seen Zach. And then you were snatched. All because I was jealous, because I thought you wanted to be Connor's best friend and not mine. If I hadn't been such an idiot, I wouldn't have put your life at risk."

Michael sighed. "Jeremy. It *wasn't* your fault. You played a prank on Connor. But you weren't the one who grabbed us. We were trespassing on their land anyway. I'm sure Kat would've grabbed us at some point."

I didn't answer. Maybe he was right.

"Jeremy. You're my best friend. You don't need to be jealous or suspect other people of plotting to steal me away. But just because we're best mates, it doesn't mean we can't have other friends too."

I nodded. It was the same thing Nazirah had said. And it was true.

"Okay," said Michael, "so we may have been in danger and you almost got thrown down a giant hole in the ground, but we actually did something amazing this week. We solved a mystery, we helped put a horrible woman in prison, and we saved a beautiful part of Scotland from being turned into a poisonous gas farm. Yes, it was dangerous, but it was all worth it, wasn't it?"

I sighed, nodding once more. It was a great relief to have Michael back, knowing that we really *were* best friends. And he didn't blame me for what happened. Connor too seemed to be my friend now. He was sitting behind us with his cousin. Zach had decided not to work at Glenkilly Castle anymore. He said he'd probably find a new job, leading ghost walks around Oxford or Derby or Sutton-in-Ashfield. I'm sure it would suit him perfectly.

"Jeremy saved my life," I heard Connor saying to his cousin on a number of occasions. Which stirred a mix of emotions in me: pride, guilt, relief.

I also heard Mr Hopton vow never to go on a school camping trip again, which is probably for the best. Mrs Dodd tried to start a round of *'If you're happy and you know it, clap your hands.'* But only Leah Ford joined in. *The Girly, Whirly, Twirly Gang* sat on the back row, scowling and cursing about Kat's nighttime antics. Imogen looked particularly embarrassed about the fact that the "monster" had been nothing more than a weird woman in fancy dress.

The coach then made a loud hissing sound as the doors closed and the driver released the handbrake. The vehicle jutted forward, with Hamish waving us off from the car park. Once the camp leader learned about Kat's attempts to terrify every child in sight, he'd been busy making phone calls to some Lord who owned the castle, explaining why things had gone downhill lately. He looked as stressed as Mr Hopton, his orange skin practically fading to a sickly yellow.

As the coach crawled slowly along the drive that led out of Glenkilly Castle, I thought back to all the times I said I'd seen a monster in the woods and how upset I'd been that nobody believed me. Well, I guess they were all right. I didn't actually see a monster in the woods. But I *had* seen something.

And then, just as the coach approached the gates that would finally exit us from the estate, I swear I saw something again… something moving through the woods. It must have been the wind, twisting branches into deceitful shadows and playing tricks with the light, because I knew for a fact that the police had confiscated the antlered head.

I narrowed my eyes, trying to focus as I stared hard into the woods. Something was definitely moving. Walking upright.

I checked to see if I could see any black Reebok trainers. But no. I only saw hooves… and antlers protruding from a hairy animal's face.

It couldn't be… could it?

Daniel Henshaw is the author of 'The Great Snail Robbery', 'The Curious Case of the Missing Orangutan', 'Jeremy's Shorts' and 'Glenkilly', all starring Jeremy Green. Daniel is a qualified **primary school teacher** and holds a **degree in English Studies**.

In 2016 one of Daniel's unpublished stories was shortlisted in the 'Best Novel for Children' category at the **Wells Festival of Literature**. He lives in **Derbyshire** with his girlfriend and two cats, Morse and Thursday.

FOLLOW DANIEL HENSHAW

 ON TWITTER: @AUTHORHENSHAW

 OR AT WWW.FACEBOOK.COM/JEREMYSNAILS

FRACKING FACTS

1. Fracking kills animals!

Robert E. Oswald, a Professor at Cornell University, studied the
effects of fracking. In one case, an accidental release of
fracking fluids into a pasture near a drilling operation resulted in
17 cows dead within an hour! Exposure to fracking fluids in
pastures or streams led to pregnant **cows producing stillborn
calves** and **goats exhibiting reproductive problems**. Of the
seven cattle farms studied, **50 percent of the herd was
affected by death or failure to breed**.

Source: EcoWatch

2. Fracking contaminates water!

According to the British Geological Survey, "Groundwater may
be **contaminated by extraction of shale gas**."
In England, groundwater supplies **a third of our drinking
water.**

Source: Friends of the Earth

3.Fracking effects human pregnancy!

A study looked at almost 11,000 women with newborns who lived near fracking sites and found a **40% increased chance of having a premature baby** and a **30% risk of having the pregnancy be classified as "high-risk."** Contributing factors include air and water pollution and stress from the noise and traffic (1,000 tankers/well on average).

Source: Forbes

4.Fracking triggers earthquakes!

57 earthquakes were detected during a two-month period in Lancashire in 2018 when Cuadrilla was fracking there.

Source: FriendsoftheEarth.uk

5.Fracking makes water flammable!

A scientific study has linked hydraulic fracturing with a pattern of drinking water contamination so severe that **tap water can be lit on fire**. The research found that levels of flammable **methane gas in drinking water wells increased to dangerous levels** when those water supplies were close to natural gas wells.

Source: ProPublica

NOTES FROM THE AUTHOR

It all started with a school camping trip.

Beaumanor Hall, Leicestershire. May 2017 (one month before The Great Snail Robbery was released).

As the sun set, draping the Leicestershire countryside in a blanket of inky shadows, my colleague, Janet, decided that we were taking the (forty or so) children on a 'night walk'… into the pitch-black woods. The kids were already anxious, shivering and whimpering – with nothing but shaky torches to guide the way (sounding familiar?) – when Janet asked me to tell them a ghost story.

"I told one last year," she confessed, "but it wasn't very scary."

"But I don't know any ghost stories," I admitted.

Janet snorted. "Call yourself an author?"

Well – that was it! Now I *had* to prove my worth!

I'll tell the scariest ghost story these children have ever heard!

I'll show Janet!

As we ventured deeper into the dark woods, I racked my brains for ideas and quickly came up with some seriously spooky stuff. When we came to a clearing in the woods, the (already terrified) children sat on logs and listened to my ghost story… the scariest tale ever told! I *really* got into it, totally lost in the story. And by the time I'd finished, I glanced around the shadowy woods… to see forty petrified children, all crying their eyes out. The other staff members glared at me, as if to say, *'What did you do that for?'* What *did* I do that for? The children sobbed through the night, into the next two days, and many wanted to go home.

Okay, so I got it drastically wrong and I felt terrible – guilty – for weeks on end. But, much to my surprise, school received no complaints about my ghost story and (eventually) we all laughed about it… and (eventually) it became the trigger for this book.

What if, I thought, *someone scares the kids with a story in the woods… but there actually is something in the woods.*

Around the same time, I watched a documentary called *'Gasland'.* If you've finished *Glenkilly* and are interested in the environmental issues raised, I recommend watching it. At the time of writing this, the movie is available to stream for free on YouTube.

So, anyway, thanks Janet!

I started writing *Glenkilly* in January 2018 and the story has gone through so many different versions, I've lost count. Numerous scenes and characters have been cut: an ancient caretaker, who Jeremy thought was a ghost (I liked him but he didn't fit the story); a crumbling service station, where an old lady tells the boys not to visit Glenkilly Castle and where Jeremy gets hit by a bus; a scene where Kat (originally called Natasha throughout – can you guess why?) gave the children 'Nature Names', which was funny but added nothing to the story. Nazirah was originally a boy, Connor was named Jarrad and the whole story revolved around the kidnapping of Imogen Rutherford, which was a great story but the version I'd written was too unrealistic and didn't work.

So thanks to the many, many, many people who've given me feedback about the story (at whichever stage you read it): Debbie Foster (MASSIVE, MASSIVE THANK YOU!!!), Ruth Simmons (now Roberts), Matt Henshaw, Ste Holmes, Sandra Glover (author of *Nowhere Boy*, *Hairy Horror* and *The Girl Who Knew*) and Llinos.

Thanks to my mysterious internet Beta Readers: Lori Weaver, Geoffrey Moehl, Sam Eckford, Breck Harding, Kristin Stamper, Justin Brown, Anna and Bobby from Toronto, Rhiannon, Dexter and Dylan De Wreede, Jennifer Anderson and her crew in New Zealand, and Somabia and Nyle in Basingstoke.

Thanks to all the children and grown-ups who I've met during School Visits (get in touch to book yours now) around the UK – and especially thanks to everyone at Annesley Primary School (staff, parents, children, past and present) for your ongoing support. And thanks to all of the Mr Hoptons and Mrs Dodds out there, doing their best every day to give children the best possible start to life. Thanks to everyone who has written reviews (**please remember to review Glenkilly on Amazon and GoodReads**), shared my social media posts and been generally supportive of my work.

Massive thanks to Jim Rogers for another AMAZING cover.

But most of all, thanks to Charlie-Fern, who has had to suffer reading/hearing this book over and over again for the past two and a half years, and also puts up with me being weird on a daily basis. You are the best human I know.

HAVE YOU READ DANIEL HENSHAW'S OTHER BOOKS YET?

FOLLOW DANIEL HENSHAW

ON TWITTER: @AUTHORHENSHAW

OR AT WWW.FACEBOOK.COM/JEREMYSNAILS

DANIEL HENSHAW

AUTHOR DAY & KS2 MYSTERY WRITING WORKSHOPS

Daniel also visits schools! Most recently he's been to…

London: Gordon Primary; **Liverpool**: Springwood Heath Primary;

Cheshire: Adswood Primary; **Northamptonshire**: Beanfield Primary, Oakley

Vale Primary; **Nottinghamshire**: Robert Mellors Primary, Wainwright

Primary, Samuel Barlow Primary, Hawthorne Primary, Mount Primary;

Brinsley Primary, Annesley Primary, Morven Park Primary, Dalestorth

Primary, Kirkby Woodhouse Primary; **Derbyshire**: Hady Primary, Tansley

Primary, Loscoe Primary, Horsley Woodhouse Primary, Coppice Primary,

Wirksworth Junior, Ashbourne Hilltop Primary

"Daniel's whole school assembly was exciting and funny. He

did exactly what we had hoped, capturing the children's

imagination and really inspiring them for a day of writing

mystery stories."

Robert Mellors Primary School, Arnold, Nottingham

If you're interested in this opportunity, email:

mrdhenshaw@gmail.com for details.

Printed in Poland
by Amazon Fulfillment
Poland Sp. z o.o., Wrocław

59458432R00188